SHOCK FOR THE
SECRET SEVEN

Enid Blyton's

Shock for the Secret Seven

Illustrated by Dorothy Hamilton

AWARD PUBLICATIONS LIMITED

ISBN 0-86163-535-3

Text copyright © Darrell Waters Limited
Illustrations copyright © 1991 Award Publications Limited

Enid Blyton's signature is a trademark of Darrell Waters Limited

First published 1961 by Hodder and Stoughton

This edition first published by
Award Publications Limited, Spring House,
Spring Place, Kentish Town, London NW5 3BH

Photoset by Rowland Phototypesetting Limited
Bury St Edmunds, Suffolk

Printed in Hungary

Contents

One

Secret Seven meeting, everyone!

'WHEN are you having a meeting of the Secret Seven again?' asked Peter's mother.

'I don't know. Why, Mother?' asked Peter, looking up from his book.

'Well, because if you do, I don't think you ought to meet in that old shed of yours,' said his mother. 'It's such very cold weather. You'd better meet up here in the house.'

'Oh *no*, Mother,' said Janet, joining in. 'It wouldn't be a *secret* meeting then. We *must* meet in the shed.'

'Well – you'll have to heat it up a little then,' said Mother. 'I can't have you down with colds just at the end of the Christmas term. Can't you do without meetings till after Christmas?'

'Not very well,' said Janet. 'We'd half thought it would be a good idea to take the Christmas presents we're making down to the shed – all seven of us, I mean – and have a sort of Making Presents meeting. We thought we could all wear our coats.'

'You'd be frozen!' said Mother. 'I'll lend you my new little Safety-First stove – even if it's knocked over, it's safe! Then I shan't be afraid of the shed catching fire.'

'Oh, *thank* you, Mother!' said both children together, and Scamper the golden spaniel barked loudly, as if he thoroughly agreed. Janet grinned. 'He say's *he'll* be jolly glad of a stove too,' she said. 'He's a real old lie-by-the-fire these days – aren't you, Scamper?'

'Well, you should take him for a good long walk,' said Mother. 'He'd love that. You're getting fat and lazy, you two!'

She went out of the room, and Janet and Peter looked at one another. 'What with exams and one thing and another we haven't really had much time for the Secret Seven,' said Peter. 'It *would* be nice and cosy in the shed with that stove – we could take all the Christmas things we're making, and do them down there – and not have to keep taking them off the table just because meals have to be laid.'

'We'll tell the others tomorrow,' said Janet, happily. 'We shall have to have a new password – it's so long since we had a meeting. What shall we have?'

'Custard pudding!' said Peter, grinning.

'What an idiotic password!' said Janet. 'Why not ham and eggs? Or toad-in-the-hole – or . . .'

'*Toad-in-the-Hole* – that's rather a good one!' said Peter. 'It'll make the others laugh. Jolly good, old girl!'

'Don't call me "old girl",' said Janet. 'I keep on telling you not to. You sound like Uncle Bertie. He always calls Auntie "old girl".'

'All right, young girl,' said Peter. 'Toad-in-the-Hole – ha, nobody will forget that! Let's see – that's sausage in batter pudding, isn't it?'

'Of course it is!' said Janet. 'How can you forget that, seeing that last time we had it, you ate four "toads" – four sausages, and felt jolly sick afterwards.'

'So I did,' said Peter. 'Scamper – the password is Toad-in-the-Hole. Don't forget!'

'Wuff!' said Scamper, and wagged his tail.

Next day at school Peter called Colin, Jack and George into a corner. 'Secret Seven meeting on Saturday at ten o'clock in the shed,' he said. 'The password is "Toad-in-the-Hole". You know – sausages in batter.'

'What a password!' said Jack. 'I'll never re-member such a silly one. I'll have to write it down.'

'No, don't. That awful sister of yours, Susie, might find your notebook and see the password,' said Peter.

'All right. I'll try and keep it in my head. I'll make up a rhyme about it – that'll help me to remember it,' said Jack. 'Let's see – Old King Cole was a jolly old soul, his favourite dinner was Toad-in-the-Hole! Ha – I'll remember it all right now.'

'You heard the time of the meeting, didn't you?' said Peter. 'You look a bit scatty this morning.'

'Well, I feel it,' said Jack. 'What with exams and things – and preparing for old Bony – he's coming to stay with me, you know – and . . .'

'Old *Bony* – who on earth is he – a skeleton or something?' asked Peter, with much interest.

'Idiot! He's a French boy – the one I went to stay with in France last year,' said Jack. 'His name is Jean Bonaparte – no relation of the great general! He's – well, he's awfully serious and earnest, and I can't say I'm much looking forward to his coming. I'm hoping Susie will like him and take him off my hands. She rather fancies herself with foreigners.'

'Don't you tell Susie anything about the meeting on Saturday,' said Peter. 'You pack her off somewhere with Bony.'

'I suppose you wouldn't let me take him to the meeting?' asked Jack, not looking very hopeful. 'I mean – Mother's sure to say I can't leave him alone on Saturday – he's coming on Friday, you see, and it will look a bit rude to rush off by myself the very next morning.'

'You don't seem very *keen* on coming to a Secret Seven meeting,' said Peter.

'Don't be stupid! Of *course* I want to come – but my mother isn't like yours. She doesn't think the Secret Seven is at all important. But I WILL come if I possibly can,' said poor Jack, looking scattier than ever.

'All right. But don't you let Susie know, now –

and DON'T tell her the password,' said Peter, sternly. 'I hope you've not forgotten how she and Binkie, that awful giggling friend of hers, once got into our shed before a meeting, and locked the door on the inside so that *we* couldn't get in – and asked US for the password!'

Jack gave a sudden grin. 'Yes. It was *awful* of them – but honestly it had its funny side. All right – I won't give our meeting away. Trust me! I'll come somehow, even if I have to park Bony in an ice-cream shop and buy him half a dozen ices to keep him quiet! By the way, tell me the password again, Peter.'

But Peter had gone. Bother – what *was* that password now – Old King Cole? Sausages? Dinnertime? Jack went off frowning. What with his sister Susie, and exams, and Christmas looming up, *and* Bony, life was very, very difficult!

Two

Password, please!

WHEN Saturday morning came, Peter and Janet were very busy. They carried the Safety-First stove down to the shed, and Mr Parks, the gardener came in to light it for them. He looked round the shed.

'Ha – you've let it get pretty messy, haven't you?' he said. 'Wants a good clean, that's what it wants. Waste of a good shed, this, that's what *I* think.'

'It *isn't* wasted,' said Peter. 'We use it for our meetings. You know we do.'

'Fat lot of meetings you've had lately,' said Mr Parks, grumpily. 'Last month I wanted this shed for my onions, and what happened? No sooner did I put them in than I had to take them out – because you wanted it for a meeting!'

'*We* took them out, Mr Parks, not *you*!' said Janet, indignantly. 'You didn't have to move a single one!'

Mr Parks gave one of his grunts, and walked out. Scamper stared after him, his tail down.

'Cheer up, Scamper,' said Janet. 'The gardener always thinks this shed is his, not ours. Peter, let's make Mr Parks something for Christmas – he's not a bad sort really, though he *is* grumpy. Remember how he gave us apples to store in the shed in the autumn?'

'Yes. But we've eaten them all,' said Peter, looking hopefully up to a shelf. 'No – there's one left, all brown and shrivelled. I say – doesn't that stove make the shed nice and warm? Buck up and tidy round, Janet. I'll put out the boxes to sit on. Did you remember your badge? Oh, yes – you're wearing it. I hope the others will all remember theirs.'

'Wuff-wuff!' said Scamper.

'All right. I know you've lost yours, scrabbling after rabbits,' said Peter. 'Janet will make you another one when she has time.'

'Wuff!' said Scamper, again, and lay down by the stove, his tail wagging just a little. He was looking forward to seeing all the Secret Seven again!

'Almost ten o'clock,' said Peter, looking at his watch. 'Now – are the others going to be late?'

They sat down on the boxes to wait for them. The door, with its big S.S. on it, was fast shut. Footsteps came up to it at last, and someone knocked loudly.

'Peter – what's the password?' whispered Janet, suddenly. 'Was it – was it Sausages?'

'Be quiet,' said Peter, and then yelled out loudly to the knocker. 'Password, please!' Jack's voice answered.

'Peter, I've forgotten it. I just know it had something to do with dinner. Is it Roast Beef?'

'No.'

'Well – is it Fried Bacon and Eggs?'

'No. Go home if you can't remember it.'

15

Janet nudged Peter. '*I* forgot it, too, you know. Let him in!'

'Against the rules!' said Peter, sternly.

'Well – is it Old King Cole?' asked poor Jack.

'No, it is NOT!' said Peter. Then more footsteps were heard, and Peter called out again. 'Password, please.'

'Toad-in-the-Hole!' came the answer in a girl's voice. Peter swung open the door – and in stepped Susie, Jack's sister, with a very skinny-looking boy behind her!

'SUSIE! Get out! You don't belong to the Secret Seven! How did you know the password?' shouted Peter, very angry indeed.

'I heard Jack saying it over and over to himself two days ago,' said Susie, smiling wickedly. 'And . . .'

'Jack – you gave our password away – and you told Susie about our meeting!' cried Peter, in a great fury.

At that moment all the others came up in a bunch, and stood amazed at the sight of a furious Peter at the door of the shed, a white-faced Jack, a grinning Susie, and a skinny boy they didn't know!

'What's up?' said George. 'And who's this? A new member?' He looked at Bony, who gazed back at him owlishly through big glasses.

'My name is Jean Baptiste Bonaparte,' said the French boy, and bowed most politely from the waist. 'I stay with my good friend, Jacques. His good sister, she bring me here. I thank you.'

There was a short silence. Nobody knew quite what to say. Then Colin spoke up. 'Look, I don't really know what's going on, but for goodness' sake ask us into the shed, Peter – it's freezing out here. I can't even *feel* my nose!'

Everyone surged into the shed without waiting for an invitation – Susie and the French boy too! That was too much for Peter.

'Look here – this is supposed to be a secret meeting!' he shouted. 'Susie, get out and take Bony or Skinny or whatever his name is, with you. Go on – you don't belong to the Secret Seven.'

'Well – I'm afraid my mother will be *most* annoyed about this,' said Susie, her nose well up in the air. 'When Jack told her he couldn't play with Bony because you had said he must come to the meeting, Mother said all right, he could go, but he must take Bony too. He wouldn't take him – so *I've* brought him.'

'Well, you just take him away again!' said Peter. 'Do you hear? Take him away. And you can go too, Jack.'

'No!' said Janet, at once. 'You're to stay, Jack. You're a Secret Seven member. Stay!'

Three

Peter loses his temper

THE poor French boy looked scared to death, and hurriedly backed away down the path to the front gate, bowing most politely all the time. Susie went with him, apologizing to him at the top of her voice, so that all the others could hear.

'I'm so sorry, Bony, but I'm afraid Peter has *no* manners at all. You really *must* excuse him, he's never *really* learnt how to behave!'

'I'd better go with them,' said poor Jack. But Peter pulled him into the shed and banged the door so violently that the noise made Scamper leap up and bark loudly.

'Now don't *you* begin being a nuisance!' said Peter to him, in such a loud voice that Scamper crept away, scared. Then Peter turned on Jack.

'How DARE you let Susie know the password? How *dare* you let anyone know we'd a meeting here today? And WHY aren't you wearing your badge? You don't DESERVE to be a member of the Secret

Seven! And FANCY bringing that awful boy here!'

'I *didn't* bring him here. Susie did,' said poor Jack. 'And how was *I* to know she was listening at the door of my bedroom when I was trying to learn the password by saying it over and over to myself? And I *haven't* forgotten my badge. I didn't wear it in case Susie saw it and followed me. She always knows I'm going to a Secret Seven meeting when I put on my badge. Look, I've got it here in my pocket! Anyway, I had to tell Mother I was going – she wanted to know why I couldn't play with Bony. And don't you glare at me like that!'

'I'll glare at you all I like!' said Peter. 'I tell you, you don't deserve to be . . .'

'All right, all right. You've said that already,' said Jack, glaring back. 'If I don't *deserve* to belong, I *won't* belong! I'll resign! I'll walk out! Here's my badge – take it, or I'll throw it away. I don't want it any more. I can't HELP having a sister like Susie, can I? Well – now you can be the Secret SIX! Goodbye!'

He took his badge out of his pocket and threw it down at Peter's feet. Then he walked out of the door, his head high, ashamed of the sudden tears that came to his eyes. To leave the Secret Seven was the hardest thing Jack had ever done in his life!

Nobody stirred. They were all too shocked by

Jack's sudden and surprising outburst. Peter stared at the fallen badge, not knowing what to do or say.

But Scamper knew what to do! He tore out of the door, barking as if to say 'Come back! Come back!' He ran round Jack's feet, and leapt up to lick him. But Jack pushed him away.

'No. Get down. You're not my friends any more.'

Scamper ran back to the shed, with his tail well down. He looked round at the others with big brown eyes, hurt and bewildered. Janet put her arm round him, and turned to her brother.

'Peter. You aren't going to let Jack go, are you? You *know* it wasn't his fault.'

Barbara suddenly burst into tears, and began to sob loudly. Peter stared at her angrily.

'Oh, don't be such a baby, Barbara, for goodness' sake! I'll ask Jack to come back, of course – but he shouldn't have lost his temper like that.'

'You lost yours,' sobbed Barbara. 'This is the f-f-f-first t-t-t-time we've ever qu-qu-qu-quarrelled. I don't l-l-like it.'

'Let's write a note to Jack,' said Colin. 'Let's tell him we can't do without him. Let's say we're sorry. Come on, Peter. You did go on at him, you know – and honestly, it's not his fault that . . .'

'I *know* it's not his fault that his sister is such a

nuisance,' said Peter, who was now feeling very uncomfortable indeed. 'All right, we'll write a note – at least, *I'll* write it, and we can all sign it. Will that do? I'm sorry I lost my temper, I really am – but Susie's enough to make anyone see red. Fancy having the nerve to bring that skinny fellow, Bony, to a Secret Seven meeting, too.'

'She simply isn't afraid of anything or anybody,' said Pam. 'It's a pity really she doesn't belong to the Secret Seven, she's really very clever, you know, and . . .'

'Belong to the *Secret Seven*!' said Peter, exploding again. 'What a thing to say, Pam! Just shut up if you can't think of anything better to say!'

'There you go again – losing your temper!' said Barbara, sticking up for Pam. 'Come on, now, Peter – what about that letter to Jack? Let's do it now. I wouldn't be able to sleep tonight if I thought poor old Jack didn't belong to the Secret Seven any more.'

Peter sent Janet to the house to fetch some writing-paper. He felt ashamed of himself. He hadn't *meant* to say all that to Jack – but that Susie, that awful sister of his – well, he'd better not think of her any more, or he'd lose his temper all over again!

Soon Janet was back with writing-paper and an envelope. Solemnly they discussed what to say. In the end Peter wrote a short and apologetic note, signed by everyone.

He read it out to the others.

'Dear Jack,

'Please don't let's make mountains out of mole-hills. I'm awfully sorry for what I said. You know we can't do without you! We can't POSSIBLY *be the Secret Six. We're meeting again tomorrow evening, at six. Please come. I'm enclosing your badge. We* ALL *want you back.*

'From

'PETER, JANET, PAM, BARBARA, COLIN, GEORGE.'

'Sounds all right,' said George. 'I bet he'll be glad to get it.'

'Scamper must sign it too,' said Janet. She rubbed some ink on the underneath of the spaniel's paw, and pressed it down on the paper, under their own signatures.

'There!' she said. 'Jack will know that Scamper agrees about this too. Peter, who's going to take the note? It ought to go at once.'

'I'll take it,' offered George. 'I go by his house.

I'll drop it in.'

'Well, be careful Susie isn't lying in wait for you,' said Peter, licking the envelope. 'Here you are – and remember, everyone – meet here tomorrow evening at six o'clock. The password had better be the same as today, as Jack won't know any new one – and I daren't put one in this note, in case Susie gets hold of it. Remember now – Toad-in-the-Hole!'

'Right,' said George, and took the note. 'Let's hope we'll be the Secret SEVEN again tomorrow!'

Four

A shock for the Secret Six

THE next evening, which was Sunday, Janet and Peter went down to the shed again. Peter was a little subdued, and quite determined to be as good-tempered as Janet always was. They set the shed in order, and Janet put some little chocolate buns on a plate – a present from her mother.

'Mother doesn't know a thing about the quarrel,' she said, 'and I hope no one ever tells her. She's rather surprised we're holding another meeting so soon, though!'

'Scamper, sit down,' said Peter. 'You seem very restless tonight.'

'I think he's remembering how you and Jack shouted at one another yesterday,' said Janet. 'He's not used to us quarrelling. I think he was quite scared.'

'Silly old Scamper,' said Peter, and patted the soft, silky head. 'DEAR old Scamper – what should we do without you?'

Bang-bang! That was someone at the door already – yes, Pam and Barbara together. They whispered the password through the door. 'Toad-in-the-Hole.'

The door opened and they went in, beaming. 'Aren't we nice and early? Hasn't Jack come yet?'

'No. Not yet,' said Janet. 'Perhaps he'll come next!'

But no – George and Colin came next – knocking loudly at the door, and saying the password together. Peter opened it.

'Oh – I hoped Jack would be with you,' he said. 'He's not here yet. Well – it's not *quite* six o'clock. He'll be along in a minute. Find a box and sit down.'

Somehow they all felt rather nervous of facing Jack. They patted Scamper and talked about Christmas, and all of them listened for Jack's footsteps.

'Ah – there he is!' said Peter, as the patter of feet was heard at last. 'Toad-in-the-Hole' said a voice outside the door. Peter swung it open, beaming.

But it wasn't Jack! It was *Susie*! Her voice and Jack's were very much alike! She stood there, stern-faced, and thrust a note at Peter.

'Here you are,' she said. 'Read this. You deserve all it says!'

She pushed the note into Peter's hand and disappeared at once into the darkness. Peter shut the door, feeling a little dazed. 'I'll open it,' he said, and slit the envelope.

'Read it out,' said Colin. And Peter, his voice shaking a little, read it to the others.

'Dear Secret Six,

Thank you for your note and apology from Peter. Sorry, but there's nothing doing. I've finished with you. I'm forming a club with Susie, Binkie, Bony and three others – we'll be the Secret Seven – and you'll be the Secret Six.

JACK.'

There was absolute silence after Peter had finished reading the note. Nobody knew what to say. Nobody particularly *wanted* to say anything. They sat staring at one another in such a peculiar silence that Scamper became scared.

He crept over to Janet and put his nose into her hand. She broke the silence with a sudden sob. 'Oh, Scamper – do *you* feel miserable, too, like us?'

'Peter! Peter! Jack can't mean it!' said George, finding his voice. 'He *can't* want to make a Secret Seven club with Susie and Binkie and Bony – and –

who else? What shall we DO?'

'Get someone else in so that *our* club is *still* the Secret Seven!' said Peter. He crumpled up Jack's letter. 'Jack doesn't care tuppence about us. I bet he's glad to leave us and make a new Secret Seven. But *why* did he have to call it the *Secret Seven*? He knows – he knows that's *our* special name!'

'Well – we can't have *two* Secret Seven clubs going,' said George. '*We'd* better be the Secret Six – what's it matter if we're Seven or Six? And the letters S.S. will do for Secret Six badges just as well as for Secret Seven. We shan't need to alter them.'

'Put it to the vote,' said Colin. 'We've got to do something about it, or else break up the club altogether.'

The idea of breaking up was too much for anyone. 'We'll vote!' said the girls, and the boys agreed. So very solemnly they voted and agreed that their club was now the Secret Six.

'Let's not go on with this meeting tonight,' said Janet. 'It doesn't seem right without old Jack. Let's break it up, and meet again some other time.'

Some other time? When would that be? Nobody said anything about another meeting, and day after day went by, and the Secret Six did not meet at all. Peter's mother was surprised.

'Aren't the Secret Seven meeting again soon?' she asked. 'I hope you haven't quarrelled!'

'Oh, I expect we'll meet again *after* Christmas, Mother,' said Peter, going very red. 'You see – well – we're all pretty busy now!'

Susie was busy too! She had told her friend Binkie all that had happened, and how Jack had left the Secret Seven. So *we'll* be the Secret Seven!' she said. 'You and I and Jack – that's three – and Bony, his French friend – that's four – and we'll choose three others. Don't look so miserable, Jack – we'll back you up. You shall be the leader!'

At first, Jack, feeling bitter about the quarrel, agreed with everything they said – but when he found that the extra three were all to be girls, he shook his head.

'No,' he said. 'I've changed my mind. I don't want to belong to any more clubs. The Secret Seven was a fine club, and there couldn't ever be a better one. I don't want to be in another club. Don't worry about it, Susie.'

'WELL!' said Susie, in a fine rage. 'After all our sympathy, and all we've done for you, you just turn round and say "No thank you; I've changed my mind." All right then – we jolly well won't have you in our club! You can just be on your own!'

Five

Matt the shepherd has some news

CHRISTMAS came and went, with all its excitements and parties and pantomimes. Peter's mother came to him with a wonderful idea in the New Year.

'Would you like me to give a party for the Secret Seven?' she said. 'Just for you seven? You've had so many good times together, so many adventures – I'd love to give a grand party just for you!'

At first Peter and Janet felt thrilled – and then they remembered that they were only six. How could they explain that to Mother? She wouldn't approve at all. In fact, she would probably be very cross to think that Peter had been the cause of Jack leaving the Secret Seven.

'She might go round to Jack's mother about it,' said Peter, gloomily. 'And you know what it is when mothers get together. You never know *what* they will make you do.'

'Well, let's ask her to put off the club party till

after the Christmas holidays,' said Janet. 'After all, we *do* have a lot of parties and things to go to.'

So, to their mother's surprise, they said please could they wait till after the holidays before they gave a party for the club? She nodded her head at once. 'Just as you like, dears,' she said. 'I don't mind *when* you have it!'

It snowed in the New Year, and Peter and Janet and Scamper were delighted. 'Lovely!' said Janet, looking out of the window at the great smooth layer of whiteness covering the farm-fields. 'LOVELY! We can go tobogganing soon. Scamper, do you hear that? Do you remember how we took you tobogganing once and you fell over and rolled all the way down the hill in the snow, collecting it round you as you went, ending up as an enormous snowball?'

'Wuff!' said Scamper, wagging his tail. He ran to the door and pawed at it. Janet was just about to turn away from the window when she saw someone coming up the path that led to the kitchen door.

'Hello – here's Matt the shepherd,' she said. 'He looks pretty grim. I wonder what's happened? I hope there's nothing wrong with Dad's sheep, out on the snowy hills.'

Mother popped her head round the door. 'Matt

the shepherd wants a word with your father,' she said. 'Find him for me, will you?'

'He's up in one of the attics, looking for something,' said Janet, and raced upstairs. 'Dad! Dad, old Matt wants you. He's at the kitchen door.'

'Now what does *he* want?' said her father. 'I only saw him yesterday, up on the hills. I'll be down in a minute, tell him.'

Janet ran downstairs and along the stone passage to the kitchen door. Matt was still standing there, his face looking very grim indeed. He didn't even smile when he saw Janet, though he was very fond of her.

'Matt! Dad's coming,' said Janet. 'Matt, where's Shadow, your old sheep-dog? Have you left him to guard the sheep? I do like him so!'

Matt didn't say a word. Janet's father came along then, and Matt touched his hat to him.

'What is it, Matt?' asked Janet's father. 'Nothing wrong, I hope?'

'Yes, master, there is. Summat VERY wrong,' said Matt, and to Janet's horror, she heard his voice trembling. 'You know my old friend, Shadow – my dog – my fine old collie that's won so many prizes? Well, he's gone, sir. GONE!'

'*Gone?* What on earth do you mean?' said Janet's

father. 'Not dead, surely – he wasn't more than five, was he?'

'No, sir. He's been stolen. I'm sure of it. Shadow would never go far from me, except when he was rounding up the sheep. He's just GONE, GONE! I've whistled and called till the sheep all thought I was mad, and ran away from me – but Shadow didn't come. I – I didn't know what to do, so I came to you. I can't do without that dog of mine. He's like a brother to me, not just a dog.'

Janet felt the tears come to her eyes. She looked round for Scamper. Ah, there he was, sitting at the end of the stone passage. How dreadful it would be to be without *him*. Poor Matt! No wonder he had walked a mile or two over the snow to tell her father about his dog.

Janet's mother came to see what was the matter and soon the whole family, and Matt as well, were sitting in the living-room, discussing Shadow the collie.

Matt was terribly upset, and quite certain that his dog was stolen. 'That dog of mine's worth a whole lot of money!' he said. 'The prizes he wins! I could sell him for a thousand pounds, sir, but I wouldn't take ten thousand for him. No, that I wouldn't. Times he's sat all night beside me when I've been tending the sheep – times when he's run for miles to find a lost one, and come back laughing all over his face! He could laugh, that dog could. I never had a dog that was better company.'

They all let the old shepherd talk and talk. It seemed to help him – but at the end there was a deep silence. Matt twisted his hat round and round in his horny brown hands, that could be so tender with the tiny, new-born lambs, and looked at Janet's mother so mournfully that she felt she too would cry, just as Janet was doing!

'Don't you worry, Matt,' said Janet's father at last. 'I'll get straight on to the police. You're quite certain he couldn't have wandered away and lost himself?'

'What! A hill-born collie that's kept my sheep for years?' said Matt, scornfully. 'Best collie-dog I ever had too. Like a brother, he was. I *must* have him back. I'll not stay on these hills without him. I'd fret too much.'

'Right, Matt. You go back to your sheep, and I'll telephone the police right away,' said the farmer. 'Don't worry too much. Why – you may find old Shadow waiting up there for you!'

'Well, sir, if I do – and dear knows I hope you're right – I'll stand at the top of the hill there and wave my old cloak,' said Matt, and went slowly back to the kitchen door, and away over the snow.

'Oh, *Mother*!' said Janet. 'Will he get Shadow back again?'

'I hope so,' said her mother. 'But if it's a dog stealer at work, it may be very difficult.'

'Mother – will *Scamper* be all right?' said Peter, and a feeling of sudden dread went through him. 'Mother, Scamper is valuable, isn't he – a pedigree golden spaniel?'

'Yes. Yes, he is,' said his mother. 'But I don't think you need worry, dear – it would be very difficult to steal a dog living in a household, one who is under our eyes all the time. Shadow was always off and away over the hills for miles, you know. If anyone liked to tempt him with a bit of meat, he might take it, and be captured.'

'I felt so sorry for old Matt,' said Peter sadly. 'Scamper – where are you? For goodness' sake keep near us all day long – and you'd better be sure to sleep in my room at night too – and . . .'

'Oh, come now – you really needn't worry about Scamper,' said his mother. 'He would NEVER go off with a stranger.'

'Here comes Pam,' said Janet, looking out of the window. 'Gracious – she looks as miserable as old Matt. What can be the matter with *her*? Oh, I do hope she hasn't bad news too!'

They heard Pam's voice calling them. 'Janet – Peter – something dreadful's happened. Let me in quickly!'

Six

Warning – dog-stealer about!

PETER raced to the front door and opened it. 'What's the matter, Pam? What's happened?'

'Oh, Peter – you know my Granny? You know her lovely poodle – the white one that always looks as if it has a coat of snow? Well, it's been stolen! And, oh, Peter, I thought perhaps we could have a meeting about it, and see if the Secret Seven – I mean the Secret Six – can do anything to help? Granny's so upset!'

'Goodness gracious!' said Peter, pulling Pam indoors. 'We've only just heard that somebody has stolen our shepherd's dog, Shadow! He was very valuable, too. It must be the same thief. Quick – come and tell my father. He's just going to telephone the police about Shadow.'

Pam went into the living-room with Peter, still crying. She loved Snowy the poodle and had taken him for many a walk. Now he was gone! Would they ever get him back?

'Daddy, wait a minute – don't telephone the police yet. Another dog's been stolen!' said Peter, rushing up to his father. 'Pam, tell my father about Snowy.'

Pam sobbed out all she knew. 'My Granny let him out last night, about nine o'clock, as she always does – and when she called him, he didn't come in! She called and whistled and then put on a coat to look for him. But all she saw was – was – boo-hoo-hoo – was . . .'

'Was *what*?' said Peter impatiently, imagining all kinds of dreadful things.

'She saw footsteps in the snow in her garden,' sniffed Pam. 'Great BIG footprints, tramping all about. And Snowy's neat little footprints were there too – and in one place the snow was all scuffed up, as if Snowy had been dragged along. Oh, Peter, *can* the Secret Seven do anything?'

'You mean the Secret *Six*,' said Peter. 'Well, we'll certainly call a meeting about it – and about our shepherd's dog too. After all, we've solved quite a lot of mysteries – but we've never come up against a dog-stealer before. What a horrible fellow he must be!'

Peter's father listened to all that Pam said, frowning. It did look as if there was some professional dog-stealing going on in their district! *Two* dogs stolen now – and both valuable ones!

'I'll tell the police about Snowy, as well as about Shadow,' he said, and picked up the telephone receiver. In a few moments he was on to the police-station. The three children heard him giving all details to the police. Then they heard him say: 'What! THREE more dogs stolen, besides these two, did you say? Well, what are you going to do about it? A dog isn't just a dog, you know – it's a friend of the family.'

He put down the receiver, and turned to the listening children. 'Three valuable dogs besides Shadow and Snowy have been stolen,' he said. 'And in every case, there have been these footprints in the snow – large prints – the police think the fellow must be a tall, heavy fellow, who knows a great deal about dogs – or who has someone behind him who knows, and who tells him where to go.'

Tears were in Janet's eyes. She was holding Scamper close to her, as if she were afraid he might be stolen at any minute! 'Oh, Daddy – can we lock Scamper up in your room? I KNOW he'll be stolen too – he's so beautiful and good and so valuable. He's a pedigree dog, isn't he?'

'Yes – and he *is* worth a lot of money,' said her

father. 'I think perhaps we *had* better guard him carefully till the thief is caught. There's one thing – the thief will treat all the dogs well, because their value would go down, if they were ill or thin, and not worth selling.'

'But – but Scamper would be MISERABLE if someone took him away from us,' said Peter. 'He'd go thin at once, I know he would. And I don't believe he'd eat a thing. What would happen to him then?'

'Let's not worry about things before they happen,' said his father. 'Look after Scamper well, and don't let him leave your side. He's well-trained –

he's not likely to go to any strangers at all. Now, I'm expecting the police at any moment – I have to take them up to Matt's hut so that they can find out if the footprints in the snow there are the same as the others they have found.'

'We'll go with you,' said Janet. 'And we'll take Scamper. He ought to be all right with three people to look after him.'

'Yes, you go,' said her mother. 'The walk will do you good. Scamper – walkies, walkies!'

'Wuff!' said Scamper in delight, and flew to the door.

'Wait! Wait for us!' shouted Peter, afraid that Scamper would rush out and be stolen at once. 'Look, Mother, there's someone out in the yard – *he* might be the thief!'

'Don't be silly, dear – that's only the postman,' said his mother. 'Go and see if he has a parcel for me – I'm expecting one.'

Peter went to the door in answer to the postman's double knock. 'Hello, postman!' he said. 'Ah – you *have* a parcel for my mother. Do I sign for it?'

'Yes, please,' said the postman, and bent down to pat Scamper. He was a little man, with a round, smiling face, and Peter and Janet liked him very much. As for Scamper, he adored him, and frisked round him, barking in delight.

'You want to be careful of this lovely dog of yours,' said the postman, patting Scamper. 'There's a dog-stealer about you know. Old Mrs Thom's lovely dog has been taken – and Mr Cartwright's dachshund – ah, he was a beauty, he was, with a coat like silk! And Miss Downey told me this morning her little Scottie was taken last week – priceless, he was – worth goodness knows how much money! You be careful of this here spaniel of yours – don't you let any stranger feed him, or let him go off on his own.'

'We won't!' said Peter, taking Scamper by the collar. 'It would be a very, very clever thief who could get hold of our Scamper. Wouldn't it, Scamper?'

'Wuff-wuff-wuff!' said Scamper, as if he understood every single word.

Seven

Up to the hills

PETER, Janet, Pam and Scamper sat down near the fire. Pam began to cry again as she spoke about Snowy, the poodle that had belonged to her Granny.

'Peter, don't you think we could call a meeting of the Seven – I mean the Six?' she said. 'I *do* want to get back Snowy, if I can, and I know I can't by myself. I'm not clever enough about finding clues, and things like that. Please, please do call a meeting.'

'All right,' said Peter. 'I will. I'll tell the others – I'll send them a note each. You and Pam can write one each, and I'll do the other. What about tomorrow morning? Now it's holidays, it would be nicer to meet in the mornings – it's so dark at night.'

So the three sat down at the table, and wrote out neat little notes – one to Barbara, one to George and one to Colin. 'IMPORTANT. *Please meet in the S.S. shed tomorrow morning at half-past ten sharp.*'

'Seems funny not to send one to Jack,' said Pam, as she licked her envelope. 'I suppose we couldn't *possibly* ask him to come?'

'No,' said Peter. 'He's probably got together another club now, and called it the Secret Seven.'

'Well, *I* don't believe he has,' said Pam. 'I met him out the other day and he looked pretty miserable. He had that funny skinny boy with him – what's his name now – Bonaparte? Bony's a jolly good name for him. He was talking at top speed, waving his arms about like anything, and old Jack wasn't saying a single word.'

'Don't let's talk about Jack,' said Peter. 'Now – who's going to take these notes?'

'I will – on my way home,' said Pam, getting up from the table. 'And for goodness' sake, Peter, watch over your dear old Scamper. What the Secret Seven – I mean the Secret Six – would do without him, I really don't know!'

'Scamper would never, never go with any stranger,' said Peter. 'Would you, Scamper?'

'Wuff-wuff-WUFF!' said Scamper, at once.

'He said "Certainly NOT",' said Peter, and Pam looked at Scamper admiringly.

'He really *talks*!' she said. 'Well, I must be going. I won't forget to leave the notes. See you tomorrow

at half-past ten. Oh – same password as before –
what was it now? It's so long since we had the last
meeting.'

'Well – it's – er . . .' began Peter.

'Old King Cole,' said Janet.

'Sausages!' said Pam.

'No – Frog in the Pond!' said Janet, knowing
quite well it was not. 'Goodness – we're as bad as
Jack.'

'It was Toad-in-the-Hole, as you both know very
well,' said Peter, remembering. 'All right – see you
tomorrow, Pam.'

Peter and Janet spent the rest of the day watching
Scamper, making certain that he did not disappear
anywhere. If he went out of the sitting-room into
the kitchen to beg a titbit from Mrs Simmons, the
cook, they went too. If he went for a little run, he was
put on the lead at once, and guarded every inch of the
way by both Peter and Janet. If he ran into the hall
when someone came to the door, they went with
him. He was rather surprised, but very pleased.

'You know, Janet, I think one of the things we
ought to discuss at the meeting is the report saying
that the same kind of footprints are found each time
the dogs were stolen,' said Peter. 'I wish we could
get a picture of the footprints, so that we could see

the size and shape – you never know if we *might* come across them somewhere and be able to *follow* the thief.'

'Oh, *Yes*!' said Janet. 'But, Peter – won't the police be doing that?'

'Yes. But there's no reason why we shouldn't help in any tracking, is there?' said Peter. 'Listen – who's that at the front door?'

'A policeman!' said Janet. 'I expect he's come about Matt's collie. Dad said he'd take him up to Matt's hut – don't you remember?'

'Yes – of course!' said Peter. 'Let's ask Dad if we can go with him. We might take a pencil and paper and copy any footprints we find.'

'Oh, *yes*!' said Janet. 'I'll get some paper at once – and a measuring tape. Peter, ask Dad if we can go with him.'

'Yes,' said the children's father. 'You can come. Do you good to have a walk! Put your snow-boots on.'

And two minutes later Janet, Peter, their father and Cobbett the policeman all trailed up the long hill to where Matt the shepherd lived in his little hut, all among the sheep. Scamper raced with them, very happy. But Matt wasn't there.

'He's out with the sheep – looking for two or

three missing ones, I expect,' said Peter's father. 'Now he's lost his sheep-dog, he's no one to help him. I must borrow another dog for him if I can. A shepherd is lost without a good dog to help him. I reckon I'll lose a lot of my sheep if his old Shadow doesn't come back.'

'Good name for a sheep-dog – Shadow,' said Cobbett. 'Now, sir – where did Matt say the dog disappeared?'

'He didn't say,' said Peter. 'He just said he'd been stolen. I say, LOOK! Footprints! Big ones, too!'

But his father and the policeman had gone on, looking for Matt, and took no notice of Peter's excited voice. 'Where's that paper you brought, Janet?' said Peter, thrilled. 'We'll copy these prints and show them to Dad when he comes back. They might be a VERY FINE CLUE!'

Eight

Footprints in the snow

THE footprints were large and clear. They were right at the back of the hut, and looked as if someone had been standing about there.

'I bet this is where the thief stood while he waited to catch Shadow!' said Peter. 'Bother – I wish I had something flat to put this paper on. I can't draw properly standing up.'

'I'll measure the prints,' said Janet, feeling most important. She took out the tape-measure she had brought, and did a little measuring. She called the figures out to Peter, and he wrote them down. Then he went into the little hut to find something flat on which to put his paper, so that he could do a little sketch of the prints.

He came out with an old tray. He turned it upside-down, sat down in the snow just beside the footprints and painstakingly copied a print of a left foot and a print of a right foot. They really were very big!

'Jolly good!' said Janet, admiringly. 'Look, here come the others again. Let's show your drawings to them.'

Matt came slowly back with the children's father and the policeman. He looked old and sad. Janet couldn't bear to look at him. 'I hate dog-thieves, I hate dog-thieves!' she said over and over again to herself. Peter ran up to his father.

'Look!' he said. 'We found some footprints and we copied them. We found them behind Matt's shed – and we thought they must have been made by the thief when he stood out there, waiting to catch Shadow.'

The policeman took the paper at once. He looked hard at the drawings, and then he looked at Peter.

'I'm sorry, lad,' he said. 'These aren't the thief's footprints.'

'Well, whose are they, then?' said Peter, surprised.

'They belong to old Matt here,' said the policeman, with a little grin. 'Fine drawings they are, Peter – but not much use, seeing they belong to the *owner* of the dog. Take a look at Matt's prints here now in the snow – just where he's been walking. He's wearing huge old snow-shoes – bigger even than the prints you've drawn – proper shepherd's boots they are, meant for all weathers.'

Sure enough, the prints Peter had drawn *had* been made by old Matt! He nodded his head when he heard where Peter had seen them. 'Ah, yes. I stand behind the hut there when I want to count my sheep down in the valley. Them's my prints all right. See, there's even the place shown here, where the cobbler mended the sole with a patch! Them's *my* prints, not the thief's. Ah, wait till I catch him, wait till . . .'

'All right, all right, Matt, old friend,' said Peter's father, seeing that the old man was trembling. 'Take things easy now. We'll get Shadow back, don't you worry. Now come along you two – it's probably going to snow again. We'd best get back. Matt, you come along for a hot drink at tea-time – and we'll give you some in a flask to take back with you.'

'Aye, sir. Thank you,' said Matt, and turned away, his eyes roving the snowy hills, always on the watch for his beloved Shadow. When would he see him again, bounding lightly along, his eager eyes looking for his beloved master?

'Dad, how would a dog-thief entice old Shadow away?' asked Peter. 'He's very fierce, you know, if anyone goes near his sheep. I've seen him show all his teeth and growl in a most terrifying way if a tramp walks by. I shouldn't have thought *anyone* could steal a faithful old dog like Shadow.'

'He probably wasn't enticed,' said his father. 'It would be easy enough to throw down a piece of meat and leave it for Shadow to find and eat – meat with some kind of drug inside perhaps, that would send a dog to sleep.'

'Oh! How horrible!' said Janet. 'You mean that the thief would come back, and pick up the sleeping dog and take him away – in a car or something?'

'Yes. That's exactly what I do mean,' said her father. 'I asked old Matt if he had seen any strangers around, but he hadn't. He says nobody comes up to his hut except his friends – old Burton the hedger, for instance, who trims the hedges round the field – and sometimes the gardener goes up to him with vegetables – and his brother goes to see him – and the grocer's boy takes him goods once a week – and occasionally the postman calls – all people who are his friends, and whom he knows well.'

'A *hiker* might go up to his hut,' said Janet. '*He* might see Shadow and steal him by throwing down meat like you said.'

'Don't be silly, Janet,' said Peter. 'Shadow would fly at him if old Matt wasn't there. He wouldn't allow *any* stranger near the sheep – and anyway, who would hike round the country now that it's deep in snow? They'd get lost! Why, even we, who know the way well, could hardly follow the path up to Matt's hut.'

'All right, all right,' said Janet. 'I was only trying to think of every single idea I could. Actually there's only one thing we know for certain – and that is that there *is* a dog-stealer about!'

'Come along now,' said her father, impatiently. 'I want to get back. I've so much to do this morning. You keep your eyes open, and see if the Secret Seven can use their brains and track down this thief.

You've been clever enough before. Why not have a meeting about it?'

'That's JUST what we've planned!' said Peter, bounding along over the snow. 'Tomorrow morning, Dad! We're going to put our heads together, and find that dog-thief, if it takes us *weeks* to do it! Aren't we, Scamper?'

And Scamper, of course, made his usual answer – 'WUFF!'

Nine

Susie, Janet – and Bony!

THE first thing Janet thought of next morning when she awoke was that there was to be a Secret Seven meeting that day. 'No,' she corrected herself, 'I mean Secret *Six*! I shall never get used to being the Six instead of the Seven. Oh, I do WISH Jack still belonged. I do WISH he'd come back.'

She had to go to the town that morning to do some shopping for her mother. 'I'll go straightaway now, Mother,' she said. 'We've a meeting this morning you know, down in the shed – an important one – about the dog-stealing that's going on. Oh – that reminds me – where's Scamper? I haven't seen him for at least ten minutes!'

'He's out in the kitchen with Mrs Simmons,' said her mother. 'Can't you smell his meaty bones cooking? He's always sure to be out there then! Now look, here's the list, dear. If you hurry, you will be back in good time for your meeting. Are you going to take Scamper with you?'

'Only if he's on the lead,' said Janet. 'You see, that dog-thief might be hiding somewhere, Mother, watching for really good dogs.'

'Well, I hardly think he would steal Scamper in the middle of a busy shopping morning,' said her mother. 'He won't like being on the lead. Anyway, he *never* goes to a stranger.'

All the same, Janet put the surprised Scamper on the lead, and walked off with him, the basket in her other hand. When she came by the police-station she saw several people reading a notice on the board outside. She went up to see what it said. It was a list of dogs that had disappeared during the last few days!

'LOST, STOLEN or STRAYED' it began, and then came the names and addresses of NINE dogs!

'*Nine!*' said Janet. 'Two from the next village, and seven from ours; Scamper, keep to heel!'

She turned as someone called her name. 'Hello, Janet! I see Scamper isn't stolen yet!'

It was Susie, Jack's sister. She was walking along with Binkie, her friend, and Bony, the French boy. Jack was not with them.

'Hello,' said Janet, who didn't like Susie.

'How are the Secret Six?' inquired Susie. 'All well and happy, I hope?'

'I don't want to talk to you,' said Janet. 'Scamper, come to heel!'

But Scamper was straining at his lead, trying his hardest to lick the French boy's legs. Bony patted him, and Scamper went nearly mad with joy. He jumped up at him and licked his face.

'Scamper!' said Janet, in amazement. 'You've only seen Bony once, and that was for just a little while – why are you making such a fuss of him?'

'Oh, dogs *adore* Bony,' said Susie, and Binkie nodded her head. 'They go mad over him, even if they've never seen him before. *Ça, c'est vrai, mon petit, n'est ce pas*?' she added in French, turning to the French boy. He nodded.

'Oh don't show off your wonderful French in front of *me*,' said Janet. 'Scamper, stop it! You're being soppy.'

'Soppee, soppee – what is soppee?' asked the French boy, fondling Scamper's silky ears. 'He ees a *chien très beau* – how do you say?'

'Bony says he's a very beautiful dog,' translated Susie, for Janet's benefit.

'Thanks – I understand *that* much French,' said Janet. '*Will* you stop pulling, Scamper? Why on earth have you suddenly gone mad over a French boy you don't know?'

56

Two more dogs came bounding up just then, and stopped at once when they came to Bony. In a moment they were rubbing lovingly against him, pawing him, licking him.

'There you are!' said Susie proudly, just as if Bony was a very clever brother. 'See how they love him? It's always the same – *any* dog adores dear Bony.'

The skinny boy patted and stroked and spoke to the dogs very lovingly in quick French, which Susie pretended to understand, nodding her head wisely all the time. Binkie nodded too, and Janet suddenly felt furious.

'SCAMPER!' she shouted. 'Come away! You know you're not supposed to be friendly with strangers. You'll be stolen one of these days, if you're so silly.'

'Stolen?' said the French boy, looking alarmed. 'Ah *oui* – there is a – what you call it – a dog-thief here in this town. Jack, *mon ami*, he tell me so.'

'"*Mon ami*" means "my friend",' said Susie. 'Jack is his friend, you see.'

'Susie, stop speaking to me as if I was in the first form!' said Janet, her face red with rage. 'Scamper, WILL YOU come here!'

Scamper stopped fussing over Bony, and at once the other two dogs took his place, whining with pleasure as the boy patted them. It really *was* rather extraordinary. Bony said something rapidly in French as Janet walked off, and Susie translated, calling after her.

'Janet! Bony says Scamper's a valuable dog and you'd better take care of him if a dog-thief is around.'

'As if I didn't know *that*!' called back Janet, and

marched off, head in air, swinging her shopping basket. That awful Susie! Showing off like that! And that grinning Binkie friend of hers! And what an *extraordinary* boy Bony was – so skinny, so owlish – and yet how fond he must be of animals for dogs to go to him like that. It just showed how silly dogs could be – *any* of those dogs – yes, even Scamper – would have followed him for miles.

'I'll report you at our meeting this morning for behaving like that,' she said to Scamper. 'Why, if that boy wanted to steal you, you'd have let him. You are a very foolish brainless dog today, Scamper.'

Scamper put his tail down, and followed Janet meekly while she did her shopping, not daring even to pull at the lead. Why was Janet cross? Didn't she know that that boy was a dog-lover, and that every dog in the town knew it?

Janet soon finished her shopping, raced home, and looked at the clock. Was she late for the meeting? No – she had one minute to spare. She pinned on her badge and then down the garden she raced and banged at the shed door. She could hear voices inside.

'Password!' shouted Peter.

'Toad-in-the-Hole!' shouted back Janet.

The door opened, and Peter looked out crossly. 'JANET! Haven't I told you before not to yell the password at the top of your voice? Come in, idiot. You're last. We were just about to begin. Sit down. Scamper, you sit down, too, for goodness' sake, and let's begin.'

Ten

A really interesting meeting

THE six were now all ready for their meeting, Scamper too. He sat solemnly beside Peter, looking as if he might join in the conversation at any minute.

'Now this meeting has been called at Pam's request,' he began. 'We all know why. It's about this dog-stealing business.'

'Wuff,' said Scamper, hearing the word 'dog'.

'Please don't interrupt, Scamper,' said Peter, solemnly, making Barbara give a sudden giggle. 'Pam, tell us about your Granny's dog, and all details about its being stolen.'

Pam poured out the whole story, and tears began to run down her cheeks. Scamper was upset, and crept over to her, trying to lick them as they fell.

'Don't let's get upset, now,' said Peter. 'That won't do any good. We've got to discuss this subject, and see if there's anything we can do to find the thief and stop other dogs being stolen. You see – there's Scamper to think about – and all kinds of dogs in the town. And there's dear old Shadow, our shepherd's dog. We simply MUST get him back.'

'But I don't see what *we* can do!' said George. 'I mean – if the *police* can't find the thief, what chance have *we*?'

'We've solved other problems before,' said Peter. 'And anyway, children sometimes hear things and spot things that grown-ups don't. And . . .'

'But what do we *know* about the thief?' said George. 'Nothing at all! How can we find a thief we don't know anything about?'

'That's where you're wrong,' said Peter. 'We *do* know certain things about him. We know for instance that he has *very* big feet.'

'So have plenty of other people,' persisted George. 'My father, for instance. He wears size t—'

'Oh, do shut up, George,' said Peter. '*I'm* doing the talking. You can make your comments later.'

'Ha ha!' said George, in a hollow kind of voice. 'You've gone all high and mighty now. "Make your comments!" Who's going to propose a vote of thanks today, Peter? And is anyone going to . . .'

'Oh, get out, George, if you can't listen!' said Peter, exasperated. 'Don't you understand that this is a very special meeting? It might even save old

Scamper from being stolen. It might be the means of finding dear old Shadow. It might . . .'

'All right, Peter,' said George, impressed. 'Go on. I won't interrupt again.'

'I'll just briefly say what we know for certain about the thief,' said Peter. 'It's what the police told my father. They said that, judging by the big, deep footprints left in the snow by the thief – *very* large prints – the man must be a tall, heavy fellow, who knows a great deal about dogs – whether they're valuable or not, I mean. He's stealing only pedigree dogs – ones that are valuable, and can be sold for a good price.'

'But why don't the dogs *bark* when they're stolen?' asked Colin. 'Scamper here would howl the place down if anyone tried to take him away.'

'It's likely that the thief throws down meat with some sort of sleep-drug in it,' said Peter. 'The dog eats it – falls asleep in his kennel – or on the street maybe, or garden – and then the thief picks him up and goes off with him.'

'And doesn't anybody think it's strange to see someone carrying a fast-asleep dog – a big one like Shadow the collie, for instance – fast asleep in somebody's arms – or over his shoulder!' said Janet. 'I don't believe that!'

'All right. *You* think of some way to entice a dog away without bribing him or drugging him,' said Peter.

'Well, I *do* know a way,' said Janet, making everyone sit up straight in astonishment. 'I *do* know a way. Now, believe it or not, this morning when I was out shopping, Scamper suddenly went to a COMPLETE stranger, and licked him and loved him, and didn't want to come with me even when I ordered him to.'

'I don't believe *that*!' said Peter at once. 'Whatever do you mean, Janet?'

'Just exactly what I say,' said Janet, and straightaway told the meeting what had happened when she had taken Scamper shopping with her that morning, and had met Susie and Binkie with Bony, the French boy.

'You should have *seen* Scamper!' she said. 'He went all soppy and silly over Bony, whined at him, and licked him and jumped up at him – just as if he was a long-lost friend. I was really ashamed of him. Fancy going crazy over *Bony* of all people. And not only *Scamper* behaved like that. Every dog that came by was the same. And it didn't even seem to matter to the dogs that Bony talked to them in *French*!'

There was a silence after this little speech of Janet's. Everyone stared at Scamper in the greatest astonishment. He stared back, wagging his tail a little. He knew he was being talked about, and he wasn't sure if he was going to be scolded or not.

'Sounds a bit like the story of the Pied Piper of Hamelin,' said Colin, at last. 'You remember how every single boy and girl loved him and followed him? Well, this boy Bony sounds like a Pied Piper for dogs!'

'I remember a girl at school once who was like that with cats,' said Pam. 'She had only to walk down the road and the cats would come running up to her – big ones, little ones, even kittens! They all adored her, and she adored them. It was most peculiar to watch. Even our old solemn cat, Tiddles, used to wait for her to come by, and then she'd try to jump down to the girl's shoulder, purring as loudly as a . . . as a . . .'

'Motor-bike?' said George, and that made them all laugh.

'I see what you're getting at,' said Peter. 'You think these valuable dogs might not be drugged or enticed with food, but just follow a sort of Pied Piper fellow who loves dogs so much that they can't help following him. Well, I just don't believe that.

Scamper, for instance, might lick Bony all over if he *met* him – but he certainly wouldn't go *away* with him!'

'I agree with you,' said George. 'And . . .'

'Knock-knock-knock.' Someone was at the door. Peter at once thought it must be Susie and Binkie.

'Keep out! This is a private meeting!' he shouted, fiercely.

'Well – is it too private for cups of cocoa and new-made buns?' said a familiar voice, and Peter leapt up at once.

'Mother! You're great! Just what we all felt like! Come in, do. We can continue our meeting afterwards. Ooh – what gorgeous buns! Get *down* Scamper, or you'll have hot cocoa all over your nose. Thanks most *aw*fully, Mother.'

Eleven

A shock for Peter and Janet

THE six, and Scamper, set to work on the hot buns and the steaming cocoa. They felt warmed and happy and cosy. The meeting was going quite well, and everyone felt rather important, discussing how they were going to help the police to find the dog-stealer. Peter passed round the sketches he had made of footprints behind old Matt's hut, and they were much admired.

'Well – to go on with our meeting,' said Peter, when every bun was eaten and every drop of cocoa drunk. 'I think we may safely rule out the idea that the dogs are stolen by a kind of Pied Piper – that is, if the dogs are anything like *Scamper* – who would certainly NEVER follow a stranger, however much he liked him. And you must admit that *most* dogs are taught not to go with strangers, especially if they're valuable dogs.'

'Quite right,' said Pam and Colin, together.

'So we come back to the idea that somebody is

throwing down food that puts a dog to sleep when he eats it. I mean – it would be a very easy thing to do, wouldn't it? For instance, take Scamper – he might be sniffing along a hedge, and find a dollop of meat just thrown down by a passer-by – the thief. He gobbles it up at once – runs a little way – drops down asleep – and up comes the thief and takes him away. If it's done at night, nobody would see.'

'I don't much like this,' said Janet, gathering Scamper up in her arms. 'It sounds too easy for words. Scamper, for goodness' sake listen carefully, and don't let it happen to *you*!'

'Well, it seems to me that the *only* thing we can do is to use the clues that the police told my father about, and look out for anyone tall, heavily-made, with enormous feet,' said Peter. 'The police thought he was heavily-built because the footprints they found in the snow were very deep – as if the thief was a burly, heavy man.'

'Right. Then you want us to look out for someone like that, and see if we can find out anything about him – if he goes out at night, for instance?'

'Yes,' said Peter. 'But for goodness' sake don't let anyone *know* you're following them, or snooping, or we'll get into trouble. Janet, I think Scamper wants to go out. He's scratching at the door. Stop it, Scamper! Hurry up, Janet, and let him out.'

'Had I better go out with him?' said Janet, anxiously. 'I mean – he *might* get stolen!'

'Don't be silly!' said Peter. 'Stolen in daylight in our own garden, with all of us here to hear him bark? Impossible!'

Janet opened the door, and Scamper disappeared, barking in delight. The meeting went on, and after everyone had promised to keep their eyes open and report anyone acting suspiciously, or looking like the thief, Peter declared the meeting closed.

'Almost twelve o'clock,' he said, looking at his watch. 'My word, how the time goes when we talk and talk! Well, good luck, everyone – and be sure to report anything interesting.'

He and Janet walked back to the house, Peter carrying the empty cups. 'A jolly good meeting, wasn't it?' he said, 'Jack's missing something interesting – I bet he wishes he hadn't walked out on us!'

'Where's Scamper?' said Janet. 'SCAMPER! SCAMPER! The meeting's over, Scamper! Here, Scamper. Here! Come along!'

No Scamper appeared, and something cold seemed suddenly to clutch at Janet's heart. She stood quite still, and looked at Peter, fear on her face. 'Peter!' she said, in a half-whisper. 'Why doesn't Scamper come? Oh, Peter . . .'

'Idiot! I suppose you think somebody came along and cleverly stole him while we sat in the shed,' said Peter. 'Just like that! Without a bark or a whimper or a howl from old Scamper. *Really*, Janet! He's probably in the kitchen, begging for a new-baked bun.'

'Yes. Yes, of course he is,' said Janet. 'I'll go and see.'

But Scamper wasn't in the kitchen. He didn't appear at all, even when Peter yelled for him in his very loudest voice. Mother came to see what all the shouting was about.

'Mother – we can't find Scamper!' said Janet, desperately. 'He slipped out towards the end of the meeting. Mother, have you seen him?'

'I haven't seen him since I came to bring you buns and cocoa,' said Mother. 'Don't look so upset, dear – he's sure to be about. He may have gone rabbiting.'

'Not in the snow, Mother,' said Janet, in a trembling voice. 'Mother, I've a *dreadful* feeling about him. He's stolen – I know he is! Oh, Mother!'

She flung herself on her mother and cried

bitterly. 'Don't be *silly*, Janet!' said her mother. 'He's probably gone to meet your father.'

But he hadn't. He seemed completely to have disappeared! There was no sight or sound of him. He just simply wasn't to be found. Peter and Janet and their mother hunted everywhere, and called and whistled. No Scamper came running, with big silky ears flapping as he pattered along.

It was a very puzzled and unhappy family that came to the table at one o'clock. The children's father was back from his walk over the farm, and hadn't seen a sign of Scamper. 'But he *can't* have been stolen,' he said for the twentieth time. 'You'd have heard him bark if he'd been taken away by anyone. Scamper would never, never go with a stranger without a great struggle. He'd bite him, he'd fly at him!'

'Not if someone gave him drugged meat and he fell asleep after he'd eaten it, and was picked up like that,' sobbed Janet. 'You know that's what probably happened to the other dogs. The police said so.'

'Now let's think,' said her father. 'Who has been here this morning – what tradespeople have called? We'll ask Mrs Simmons.'

Mrs Simmons was startled and upset to hear that

Scamper had disappeared. 'Well, let's see now who's been here in the last hour,' she said. 'There was the grocer with his van – and Alfred and John Higgins, two little boys collecting for something – and the postman – and the laundryman and his van – and old Mrs Hughes, calling for the mending – and a man after a farm-job . . .'

'After a farm-job? *That* sounds like someone who might steal Scamper!' said Peter. 'Dad – Dad, can we trace him? Quick, Dad, ring up the police. We *must* get dear old Scamper back, we must, we must!'

Twelve

Who can have stolen Scamper?

NOBODY even thought about lunch-time – all that anyone thought of was Scamper! Where was he? Was he *really* stolen? Peter's father rang up the police at once, and asked them to keep a look-out for Scamper. 'He can't have been gone for much more than an hour!' he said.

'Stolen from your garden, you say, sir?' said the policeman. 'Have you a list of people calling at your house during the time you mention?'

'Yes – and there seems to have been quite a stream of callers – some with vans!' said Peter's father. 'A van would have been very useful. If Scamper had been popped into one, the running of the engine would have drowned his barking.'

'About this man who called for a job on the farm, sir – have you a description of him?' asked the policeman.

'Yes – I saw him myself – a little fellow with a limp. Not strong enough for farm-work.'

'Well, that rather rules him out, sir,' said the policeman. 'We think the thief is a big fellow, you know, with big feet to match.'

'Yes – well, you're probably right,' said Peter's father.

'I think the small boys who came collecting can be dismissed as suspects too,' said the policeman. 'We'll find out about the man who came inquiring after a job – just in case, sir.'

'Right. I'll see the laundry-man and the grocer,' said Peter's father. 'I don't for one moment think they're the thieves, though – we know them so well.'

'Ah, but they've each a van, sir. Easy enough to entice a dog into a van – slam the door – and drive off!'

That afternoon Peter and his father went to the laundry and asked to see the van-man who collected their dirty laundry that morning. He came out at once, and nodded to Peter, who had often ridden in his van when he was smaller.

'I hear you want to see me, sir. Anything I can do?'

'Er – did you happen to see our dog Scamper when you called this morning?'

'Well, sir, no. Don't tell me he's been stolen!'

'We're rather afraid he has,' said Peter. 'What time did you come to the house?'

'Let's see now – about quarter past eleven, and I didn't see a sign of the dog. He usually comes up wagging his tail – very good-tempered dog, sir.'

'Quarter past *eleven*! Well, he was down in the shed with *us*, then!' said Peter.

'Sorry I can't help you more, young man. I know how you feel about the dog. I'd feel the same about mine.' The man clapped Peter sympathetically on the shoulder. 'Hope you find him!'

Peter and his father went off. 'Well, it *can't* have been the *laundry*-man,' said Peter. 'I didn't think it could be. He's too nice. Let's go to the grocer's now, Dad. The grocer's man is a great big fellow – he fits the description of the thief better than the laundry-man did. He's a new man, too, Mrs Simmons says – he just *might* have taken Scamper.'

The grocer was very concerned to hear about Scamper. He called to the back of the shop. 'Reggie – come here a minute. You delivered goods at the farm today, didn't you?'

A big burly man came out, red-faced and smiling. 'Yes, sir – I did. Anything wrong?'

'This boy's dog has gone and they're afraid he's been stolen. He'd like to know if you saw the dog anywhere around when you delivered the groceries.'

'What sort of a dog?'

'A golden spaniel,' said Peter at once.

'No. I didn't see any dog at the farm,' said the man. 'Though I do recollect seeing him once or twice. Very friendly, he was.'

'Well – thanks,' said Peter's father, and walked out of the shop.

'He *might* have taken Scamper,' said Peter. 'He's the kind of man that would make heavy footprints in the snow, Dad. He's heavy and tall and has big feet.'

'That's true,' agreed his father. 'I took a look at his great feet, too. But he has such an open, honest face, Peter. And I took a look at the grocer's van, too – it was standing outside the shop. Did you notice?'

'No,' said Peter. 'Why – was there anything peculiar about it?'

'It was quite an ordinary van,' said his father, 'but it only had a roof – it was open at both ends so that goods could be easily put in and out, and . . .'

'And that means that Scamper *couldn't* have been taken away in it – he'd have jumped out – or at any rate been seen,' said Peter. 'Yes, Dad – you're right. We'll have to rule out the grocer's man. That's two people in the clear.'

'That leaves the boys who were collecting for something, the postman, and old Mrs Hughes who comes for the mending,' said his father. 'Well, I *really* think we can say the small boys had nothing to do with the matter . . .'

'I don't see why!' said Peter. 'Scamper likes children. He might quite well have gone off with them for a walk. He wouldn't go with a grown-up – but he does like children.'

'Well, look – there's one of the boys!' said his father. 'See, over there. And he has a dog with him – a terrier. Let's ask him if he saw Scamper this morning. Hey, Alfred – come here a minute. You question him, Peter. He might be scared of me.'

Alfred came over, rather shyly, his dog on a lead beside him, wagging its tail eagerly.

'Alfred – you came to the farm this morning, didn't you – with John, your brother,' said Peter. 'Did you see our dog Scamper there?'

'Yes,' said the boy. 'He came up and wagged his tail at my dog Buster here, and they rubbed noses like anything. And we got twenty pence each for our collecting-box. We collect for Sick Animals – we're very fond of animals. We've collected over five pounds now. Scamper wanted to come with us, he seemed to like Buster. I hope your dog isn't lost.'

'I hope not too,' said Peter, with a sigh. 'What time did you come to the house?'

'About half-past eleven, I think – maybe a bit later,' said Alfred.

'Thanks awfully,' said Peter. 'Well, Dad, we can rule out anyone who came before a quarter to twelve, because Scamper was about then, when those boys came. It must be someone who came between then and the time we left the meeting. That narrows it down a bit.'

'We'll go back and have some lunch,' said his father. 'We can't do much more now. If ONLY Scamper would come rushing up to meet us!'

Thirteen

A meeting about Scamper

NOBODY wanted much lunch that day, even though it was more than half an hour late! 'I can't seem to *swallow* properly,' complained Janet. 'Mother, *where* do you think Scamper is? Do you think he could have gone up to the hills to see Matt?'

'Well, no, darling,' said Mother. 'He doesn't usually rush all the way up the hills to see Matt, especially when snow is on the ground.'

'Well, we've seen one of the boys who came here this morning – and we've seen the grocer's man, and though he's big and hefty and wears large boots, *he's* not the thief. He has an open van, so if he had taken Scamper, Scamper would have jumped out or made an awful noise.'

'And we can rule out the laundry-man because he came at a quarter-past eleven and didn't see Scamper. Did you let him out of the shed by any chance?' said Mother.

'We did,' said Janet. 'He scratched at the door,

so out he went!'

'That leaves the postman, and old Mrs Hughes who came to collect the mending,' said Mother. '*Neither* of them could have taken Scamper. Mrs Hughes is absolutely terrified of dogs, and if the postman took away Scamper, everybody would have seen Scamper walking beside him, back to the post-office. I do feel it must be someone like the man who came asking for farm-work.'

'Well, I saw that fellow myself, and he didn't in the *least* fit the description the police give of the dog-thief,' said Dad. 'He was a skinny little fellow, small and underfed, with feet like a woman. He looked as if he'd run for his life if a dog so much as sniffed at him.'

'That only leaves Mrs Hughes,' said Peter.

'Well, you must know quite certainly that *that* poor old thing wouldn't steal a farthing, let alone a dog,' said Mother. 'She loves Scamper, and always brings him a titbit when she calls for the mending.'

'A titbit!' said Janet. 'Oh, Mother – do you think this morning's titbit had a sleeping-pill in it? Do you think Scamper ate the titbit and fell asleep, and Mrs Hughes . . .'

'Now *do* you imagine that that poor little old lady could *possibly* carry a heavy dog like Scamper all the way from here to the village?' said her mother. 'This is getting ridiculous. For goodness' sake, eat your lunch and be sensible. If you're going to go about suspecting innocent people, I shall be very cross.'

'Let's have another meeting and talk about the whole thing,' said Peter, seeing that Janet was near tears at being spoken to so sharply. 'If six of us talk round and round the matter, we may think of something.'

'I don't want a meeting without Scamper,' said Janet, beginning to cry. 'It's horrid not knowing who's taken him. It doesn't seem to be ANYONE who came here today, so who can it be?'

'I've a good mind to go all round the village and look for men with very large feet,' said Peter, banging the table and making everyone jump.

'Oh, don't be silly,' said his mother. 'You can't possibly go up to anyone with large feet and say "Please, have you stolen my dog? Your feet are big, so you may have done so."'

Peter just couldn't help smiling at this, though the smile disappeared almost at once. 'All right, Mother, I think I'll call a meeting and see what the others have to say. Have you finished, Janet? Hurry up, then. I'll go and see George, and we'll collect the others.'

It was a relief to have something to do. Waiting about, hoping against hope to see the beloved golden figure come padding up, tail wagging, was very upsetting. Peter went off to George's house.

'Dear old Scamper's been stolen,' he told the startled George. 'I'm calling a meeting again, at once. Please don't start sympathizing with me too much, George, else I shall howl. Will you go round and tell the others?'

'Of course!' said George, shocked. He patted Peter on the back. 'Cheer up. The Secret Six will get him back!' Off he went, and soon he had rounded up the rest of the club – Colin, Pam and Barbara. They were horrified at the news.

'There now!' said Pam. 'I was *afraid* of Scamper being stolen as soon as I heard the news that my Granny's Snowy had gone. Let's get to the meeting shed, quick!'

On the way there, they met Susie, Binkie, Bony and Jack. 'Ha!' called Susie at once. 'Going to have a meeting of the Secret Six? Have you turned anyone else out yet? I'm expecting any minute to hear you're the Secret Two!'

'Shut up,' said Pam, rudely. 'We're going to have

a most important meeting – about Scamper. He's been stolen.'

'Oh, I expect he's just run away,' said Susie. 'I would too, if I were Peter's dog.'

'SUSIE! Be quiet,' said an angry voice. It was Jack's. He called to George. 'George – is that true? Has old Scamper really been stolen?'

'Well – we're not absolutely sure,' said George, cautiously, not certain if Peter would approve of him giving information to Jack, now that he wasn't a member. 'Anyway, it can't be of any interest to you now.'

The French boy hadn't understood properly. He turned to Jack. 'He say something of a dog – what dog?'

'Le petit chien s'en va!' said Susie, fancying herself very much. *'Il est –* er *– stolen!'*

'Mais ça, c'est terrible,' said Bony, and Jack couldn't help nodding. It *was* terrible to hear that Scamper had been stolen. Whatever would Janet and Peter do without him? Jack wished and wished he still belonged to the Secret Seven – how eagerly he would have helped to try and find dear old Scamper!

'Serves Peter right!' said Susie, and was amazed to receive a really hard shove from Jack. He glared

at his sister. 'If you say that again, I'll – I'll push you into the pond!' he said. And dear me – he really *meant* it! Susie didn't dare to say one more word!

Fourteen

Something to do

EVERYONE arrived promptly for the meeting. They came to the shed in a bunch, and knocked. The password was said, and in they all went. For once, Peter didn't even look to see if everyone was wearing the S.S. badge!

'You all know that – that – the meeting's about – about poor old Scamper,' he said, giving a little choke. Pam reached out and patted his arm, tears in her eyes.

'We're terribly, awfully sorry, Peter,' she said. 'But we'll find him – we *will*. We've never failed in anything yet.'

Peter gave them a quick outline of the people who had come to the house that morning, both before and after Scamper had left the meeting.

'We ought to question every single one of them,' said George, sternly.

'Well, most of them *have* been questioned,' said Peter. 'Especially the two with vans – they could so easily have popped Scamper into a van. But we know they didn't. And the man who came after a job is in the clear, too – he was very small, my father said – and we do know that the dog-thief has large feet and must be a big man.'

'And it's not the two little boys,' said Janet. 'Anyway, they came to collect for Sick Animals, so they'd hardly steal a dog.'

'And it's not old Mrs Hughes – she's afraid of dogs,' said Peter. 'Anyway, she's an old darling. And then there's Postie, the postman. You all know *him* – he's a tiny fellow, always bright and cheery. I should think his boots are no bigger than Janet's.'

'Well, someone would have seen him with Scamper, if he *had* taken him,' said Colin. 'He has to go from house to house and heaps of people would have seen Scamper walking with him – and I just can't imagine that he *carried* Scamper – as the thief would have to do, with a dog fast asleep from drugged meat.'

'Well, if that's all the people who came to the house, and not one of them took Scamper, he MUST be somewhere around,' said Pam. 'Maybe he's hurt himself – maybe he's lying somewhere about, waiting for you to go to his help.'

'Pam – *can* you imagine Scamper lying somewhere without giving a single bark, or howl or whine?' said Peter, impatiently. 'Do be sensible. Now – has anyone any suggestions?'

Nobody had! They sat and looked at each other, trying their hardest to think of some good idea.

'Well?' said Peter, looking from one to the other. Colin was the only one to answer.

'*I'm* going to do the only possible thing,' he said. 'Something already suggested at our last meeting. I'm simply going to keep my eyes open for a heavy man with rather large feet – and follow him home. If he's the one who's taken Scamper, he'll probably have him there – and if I yell out "Scamper!" at the top of my voice, he's sure to bark – even if he can't come running out, because of being tied up.'

'It does seem to be about the only thing we can do,' said George, frowning. 'Though I've no doubt that the village will be *crowded* with big men and large feet! Well, I'm going to start this very afternoon. The sooner the better. Shall we close this meeting, Peter, and get on with the job? It will be dark pretty early today.'

'Right,' said Peter. 'But for goodness' sake don't get into trouble, any of you – I mean, don't let anyone you're following *guess* that you're tracking them.'

'Of course we won't,' said Pam. 'I'm glad we've something to *do*. It's no use sitting about moping – though I feel I could quite well cry when I begin to think about what might have happened to dear old Scamper. Oh, I *wish* he'd come scratching at the door, I *wish* he'd . . .'

'Shut up, Pam,' said George, seeing that Janet was beginning to look upset. 'Well, Peter – shall we go? When shall we report anything – *if* we have anything to report?'

'Oh, *immediately*,' said Peter. 'Either Janet or I will be at the house. Gosh – I hope someone *does* have something to report. Well, goodbye, all of you. See you again soon.'

They trooped out of the shed, and Peter shut the door carefully and locked it, putting the key under the stone as usual. He and Janet went back to the house.

'I don't feel very hopeful, do you, Janet?' said Peter miserably. 'We can't really expect to do better than Dad, or the police.'

'Well – with seven of us – oh dear, I mean *six*, of course – watching out – there's just a chance we may hit on something,' said Janet. 'I just do wish I could stop myself from expecting to see Scamper come rushing round the corner. I wonder what the others

Something to do

will do this afternoon in their search for large-footed men. I know *one* man who has the biggest feet *I* ever saw.'

'Who?' said Peter, at once. 'Quick – *who*? He might be the thief.'

'Well, he's not. He's the tall policeman that came to see Daddy!' said Janet.

The other four had walked down into the town together, talking. They split up at the station, and went their different ways. Colin said he was not going home – he was going to sit down on the seat outside the station, and watch different people go by. 'I *may* see someone who's just the type we want,' he said. 'Goodbye – and good luck! Keep your eyes open – if that thief *is* here in this village, we're bound to see him sooner or later.'

Colin sat on the seat for a minute or two, watching the passers by – and then he sat up straight. A man walked by with a heavy step – a man with outsize shoes – a burly man with a not very pleasant face. '*And* he's carrying a dog!' said Colin, in the greatest excitement. 'I'll follow him. I'LL FOLLOW HIM!'

Fifteen

Colin does a little trailing

THE large-footed man walked heavily down the street, still carrying the dog. It wriggled a little and the man put it down. It whined and dragged back, trying to get off the lead.

Colin couldn't help feeling excited. 'The dog is trying to escape,' he thought. 'And what a beauty it is – a tiny miniature poodle – must be worth a lot of money. Has he stolen it? It seems a bit rash to carry it through the town, if so, but he may have stolen it from miles away. Nobody here would recognize it, then.'

He kept as close to the man as he could. The fellow did not walk fast, but took such enormous strides that Colin had to hurry to keep behind him. The man came to the bus-stop and sat down there, on the seat for waiting passengers. Colin debated what to do. Perhaps he had better sit down too. So down he sat. The little dog whined and strained towards the boy, and the man pulled him roughly back.

'Shame!' thought Colin. 'Dragging him away from me so unkindly. I'm sure he doesn't belong to the man. People aren't rough with their own little dogs. I shall certainly go on watching him.'

After about five minutes the man got up and went on again. Colin leapt up too, and followed. The man was now carrying the dog under his arm – and then suddenly, to Colin's great surprise, he tucked the little thing right inside his coat, so that it couldn't be seen!

'Now why?' thought the boy, puzzled. 'Gracious – there's a policeman coming along – the man didn't want him to see the dog, I suppose. This is VERY, VERY suspicious! I must certainly keep on his trail.'

The man took Colin for rather a long walk – up a steep hill, down the other side, and then round and back to the town again. He put the little dog down once, for a trot, and then popped him under his arm once more.

At last he came to the gate of a small house. He set the dog down, and it at once ran up to the front door. Colin stopped near the gate and watched.

The man stood there at the gate, holding it open. He spoke to Colin.

'Do come in! You've been following me about for miles, goodness knows why. Is there anything interesting about me? Or are you practising trailing for the Scouts, or something? Pray come in! You're quite a good trailer, if rather conspicuous. And if you don't know what that word means, let me tell you that it means "easily seen". I've had my eye on you all the way, young-feller-me-lad, though you thought I hadn't spotted you. You don't by any chance want to steal this little miniature poodle, do you?'

Colin simply didn't know *what* to say. He stood there, gaping. The man pushed him through the gate and up to the front door, holding him quite firmly by the arm.

An old lady stood at the door. She had just opened it, and at once saw the tiny poodle. She picked it up and fondled it.

'Diddums enjoy his walkie-walk then?' she said, and kissed the poodle on the top of his head. 'Who's this boy, John?'

'I've no idea,' said the man, and pushed Colin in front of him. 'He has followed me very carefully for miles. Maybe he wanted to steal Diddums!'

'Oh, the wicked boy! Surely he's not that dreadful dog-thief who's been going about,' cried the old lady, and she hugged the tiny poodle to her. 'Let's call the police.'

'Oh, no – please don't!' said Colin, in great alarm. 'I'm not a dog-thief, honestly I'm not. I – I thought perhaps *you* might be, sir. It – well – you see – well, it's not often you see a *man* carrying a tiny poodle – I mean, they're really lap-dogs – dogs for women, aren't they? I – I . . .'

By this time he had been pushed into the house, and the front door was shut. Colin felt more and more alarmed.

'Please don't call the police, sir, please let me go. My father would be awfully angry with me. You see, my friend has had his golden spaniel stolen, and we're trying to find it for him. We're all of us looking out for a large-footed man, and . . .'

'And I've large feet – and was carrying a valuable dog. Well, you certainly puzzled me this afternoon. I hope you enjoyed your walk?'

'May I go please, sir?' said Colin, desperately. 'I apologize, I do really. I expect we'll make a lot of mistakes before we catch the thief.'

'I rather think you will,' said the man. 'No, I shan't let you go yet. Don't look so alarmed. I was just about to ask you to share a bottle of ginger-beer with me – with a slice or two of lemon in it. Very nice that way. Mother, will you get us some – and a few buns as well?'

Colin heaved an enormous sigh of relief. This man wasn't *really* angry, after all, and now that he could look closely at him, he saw that he had a merry twinkle in his eye. Thank goodness! Colin decided that he would be much more careful about trailing anyone in future. To think that the man had known he was behind him all the time!

He enjoyed the ginger-beer and buns, said thank you very politely, and escaped, the tiny dog following him to the door.

'Gosh!' said Colin, scurrying home. 'I've done *my* bit today. I wonder how the others are getting on!'

Well, let's find out! Pam and Barbara are off on their own – what luck have *they* had?

Sixteen

Jack puzzles his brains

PAM and Barbara had decided to work together in their task of trying to find the dog-thief.

'Two heads are better than one!' said Pam, and off they went. 'Now to look for tall, burly men with big feet.'

But alas – the tall, burly men they saw had small feet – and the only men with large feet were *little* fellows! The girls were rather surprised.

'It seems the wrong way round,' said Pam, examining the feet of an enormous coalman heaving a sack of coal over his shoulder. 'Look how tiny this man's feet are! He *ought* to wear shoes size 12 at least! He's so BIG!'

'Anything wrong with my feet, Miss?' said the coalman, astonished to have them stared at so closely. The two girls went red, muttered something and ran off. They hardly dared to examine anyone's feet after that!

They saw Colin in the distance, and decided to

walk in the opposite direction.

'No good *all* of us meeting and looking at the same people,' said Pam sensibly, and turned up a long, very quiet road that seemed to go on for miles. It ended in a lane that ran between fields. In a nearby field stood a large old rambling house, with many sheds, big and little, round it. The girls walked on down the lane – and then Pam suddenly caught hold of Barbara's arm, making her jump.

'Barbara – can you hear that noise?'

'What noise? Oh – that's only dogs barking,' said Barbara.

'*Only* dogs barking! Aren't we *looking* for dogs? Well, do you see that lonely old house with all those sheds around, set in the fields? Wouldn't that be a marvellous place to keep stolen dogs? I *bet* Scamper's there – *and* Matt's collie – *and* Snowy, my Granny's dog!'

'Oh, Pam – no – why *should* they be there?' said Barbara. 'It's probably just ordinary dog-kennels – you know, kennels kept by someone who takes care of people's dogs when they go away.'

'Well, I'm going to LOOK!' said Pam. 'And what is more, I'm going to stand outside that high fence round the place, and yell "SNOWY! SCAMPER! and SHADOW!"'

'Oh – well, that's not a bad idea,' said Barbara, feeling suddenly excited. Supposing all the stolen dogs *were* there – what a thrill it would be! What heroines she and Pam would be, too!

The two girls went boldly up to the fence. Pam asked Barbara to hoist her up, so that she could see over the top. Up she went, and gazed on a mass of small and big sheds, each with their own little yards. Dogs of all kinds and shapes were there, barking, whining, running about . . .

Pam began to shout at the top of her voice. 'SCAMPER! SHADOW! SNOWY! SCAMPER, SCAMPER!'

The dogs heard the shouts and fell silent, all of them staring across the yards at the shouting girl. Then they began to answer back – WHAT a row they made! Some were excited, some were angry, some just wanted to make a noise.

A young woman and a man came running out of the house to see what was the matter. They quietened the dogs quickly, and then saw Pam, up on the fence. The man said something to a dog by his side, and it raced out of the front gate and round the fence to the two girls, growling. Pam and Barbara were absolutely terrified. They both sat on the top of the fence, yelling for help!

The man and the girl came up, looking very

Jack puzzles his brains

angry. 'What do you think you're doing, shouting at my dogs like that?' he said. 'You be careful they don't get loose and attack you.'

'Please call off this fierce dog below us,' said Pam, beginning to cry with fright. 'We – we were only calling out the names of some stolen dogs we know, to see if any of them were here.'

'You little idiots!' said the man. 'We're dog *breeders*, not dog-thieves! Bob, leave the girls alone – down, Bob. Now you go, you two, and don't yell at our dogs again. Bob won't hurt you – he'll just see you off the field.'

Very timidly the two girls jumped down from the fence and walked past the dog Bob, and out of the field. Bob watched them sharply all the way, as if he meant to see that they didn't help themselves even to a snowball! They were most relieved to be safely back on the road again.

'I think that was rather silly of us,' said Barbara. 'Don't let's do anything like that again. Let's go to the dairy and buy ice-creams. I feel I need something like that.'

They crossed the road to go to the dairy, and Pam suddenly nudged Barbara's arm.

'Look – there's Jack, all by himself. Shall we speak to him? That awful Susie isn't with him, nor

Bony or Skinny, or whatever that French boy's name is.'

Jack had seen the two girls, but turned away. Pam called to him.

'Jack! Come and have an ice-cream!'

Jack looked surprised and pleased, but shook his head. 'No thanks – it's awfully kind of you – but – well, I'm busy.'

'We've been looking for the dog-thief,' said Barbara. 'But we've had no luck. Are *you* looking for him too – even though you're not in the club now?'

'I might be,' said Jack, cautiously. 'Well – I can't stop now. As I said – I'm busy.'

Yes – Jack *was* busy. He didn't belong to the Secret Seven – or Six – any more, but that wasn't going to stop him from looking for dear old Scamper! He had met Colin, who had told him everything he knew – told him all about the visitors to the farm that morning – the laundry-man, Mrs Hughes, the two boys, the postman, the man asking for work, the grocer's man . . . 'And not one single one of them could have stolen Scamper,' said Colin. 'Not one! The police just don't know *who* took Scamper – but they're pretty certain it's the same thief who took the other dogs, and left his enormous footprints in the snow, when he stole the dogs at night.'

And now Jack was busy on his own. What was he doing? What had he found out? How the two girls would have loved to know!

Jack had been thinking very hard since he had heard the whole story from Colin of Scamper's disappearance. The dog certainly had been stolen – there was no doubt about that – but why hadn't he barked or howled when he was taken away? That was what puzzled Jack. And why hadn't the *other* stolen dogs made a fuss too?

'The police thought that the dogs didn't make a noise because they had eaten some drugged meat, or something like that thrown down by the thief – and had fallen asleep, and then had been carried away,' thought Jack. 'But the thief must surely always have had a car or a van or lorry to pop the dog into? After all, how *could* a big dog like Matt's collie have been carried off – unless in some kind of car or van? I know the thief is supposed to be big and burly – but even so, people would notice *any* man carrying a large, sleeping dog.'

He sat on his bed and puzzled his brains for a long time. Susie banged at his door, but he wouldn't answer. Somehow, somewhere, there must be a clue that would fit this odd problem – some key to unlock the mystery.

'ALL the dogs must have known the thief, or they certainly wouldn't have eaten any food he threw down,' said Jack to himself. 'Scamper wouldn't dream of touching any food given to him by a stranger – and he definitely wouldn't go off with anyone he didn't know. He'd bark the place down! So the thief *must* have been someone that all the dogs knew – someone that every one of them trusted and liked very much – just as they love Bony and will follow him anywhere. Bother – who *is* this peculiar thief, loved and trusted by dogs everywhere? It *must* be one of those seven people who went to the farm this morning.'

He decided to go out for a walk – but that sister of his would want to go with him, and take Bony as well! Jack was getting very tired of Bony. He went to the window and looked out – no one was in the garden. He slid down the pear-tree outside and was out in the road before anyone had spotted him.

'I shall think better when I'm walking,' thought Jack, hopefully. 'Hello, there's old Mrs Hughes. *She* was one of the visitors at the farm this morning.'

Before he could go over and say 'Hello' a small dog came bounding up to the old lady. She gave a horrified shriek and tried to beat it off with her stick. Jack went to the rescue at once.

'Well!' he thought, as the dog ran off down the road, tail between its legs, 'well – it certainly was NOT Mrs Hughes who took Scamper away. I'd better take the old lady home – she's really scared!'

It was on the way to Mrs Hughes's house that Jack saw Postie, the smiling little postman, delivering letters.

'Oh, postman, I've been so scared by a little black dog,' said the old lady in her quavering voice, and Postie nodded.

'Ay, Mam – I know how scared you are of dogs. Anyone that's been bitten once IS frightened of them. I've never been bitten, and it's a good thing I'm not scared of them, for I meet so many when I'm out delivering letters.'

'Ah, but they love you, don't they, Postie?' said the old lady. 'You're kind to them. I've seen them run up to you in the street, tails a-wagging. How I wish *you'd* find that dog-thief for us.'

'I wish I could, Madam,' said Postie. 'He must be a cruel, hard-hearted fellow, that.' He went through a nearby gate to deliver a letter and at once a dog came bounding to welcome him, licking in delight.

Jack puzzles his brains

'Well, little Tim the terrier, how are you?' said Postie, and patted the excited dog, who followed him right to the house and back to the gate. Jack watched. If anyone could persuade a dog to go with him, the postman could! But he was not in the *least* like the thief. He should be tall, burly and have large feet – and he should surely have a car or a van to take away a dog.

'Now suppose Postie threw down a bit of drugged meat to *that* dog – and he ate it and fell asleep – Postie couldn't POSSIBLY carry him off over his shoulder without being seen. Everybody he met would notice the dog he was carrying, and ask him questions. I wonder if the *grocer's* man is loved by dogs – *he* had a van. No – he's been ruled out, Colin said. Well, this is a real puzzle!'

Jack suddenly decided to follow the postman, and see if all the dogs at the houses he went to made a fuss of him. So he trailed Postie, carefully keeping out of sight. Yes – every single dog belonging to any house the postman went to, welcomed him with the utmost delight.

'*Just* as if he were old Bony,' thought Jack. 'What on earth is there about Bony and Postie that makes dogs adore them? It beats me! A sort of gift, I suppose.'

Jack puzzles his brains

He trailed the postman back to the post-office, and was just about to go home, when Postie came out again. He had no post-bag this time, and he grinned at Jack.

'Hello!' he said, 'I'm off home now. Done at last. I've walked miles today! My poor feet are tired out!'

Jack didn't know where the postman lived, but he decided to see. Did he have a dog of his own? Probably he had two or three. He trailed Postie carefully, keeping out of sight, and saw him go into a small cottage not far away. A plump little woman was in the garden, taking in some washing. She was so like the postman that Jack guessed she was his sister.

'Hello, Tommy,' she called. 'Your meal's in the kitchen, and the teapot's on the hob. Help yourself! Are you going out again tonight? There's more snow forecast.'

'Yes, Liz. I've got to go out,' said Postie. 'Another delivery, you know. It'll be nice and dark then.'

Jack frowned. '*Nice* and dark.' Why '*Nice* and dark'? Why should the postman be glad of the dark? Jack shook himself. 'Don't be silly!' he thought. 'You CAN'T suspect the postman! He LOVES dogs – and they love him!'

Seventeen

Jack makes a surprising discovery

NEXT morning everyone in the town was talking about the same thing.

'ANOTHER dog has been stolen! Have you heard? It's Mr Kaye's beautiful little prize pup – his Alsatian. Only four months old, and worth a large sum of money. Goodness knows what he paid for it.'

It was Mrs Simmons at the farm who told Peter and Janet. 'Heard the latest news?' she said. 'That dog-thief has been at work again. Mr Kaye's Alsatian pup has been stolen.'

'Who told you?' said Janet.

'Postie,' said Mrs Simmons. 'He was that upset. "'Nother lovely dog gone!" he said. And he inquired after old Scamper, hoping he had come back. This is a terrible business, isn't it? No dog is safe, it seems to me. And it's always the valuable ones that go.'

Jack, too, heard the news, and frowned. Yet

another dog! A fairly big one too, although only a pup. He knew Mr Kaye and decided to go and see him.

He arrived on Mr Kaye's doorstep just as he was saying goodbye to two policemen, who had come to get particulars of the theft.

'Well, we'll do what we can, sir,' said one of the men, 'but not one of the stolen dogs have we found yet – nor even heard of. It's a very clever thief that's at work, sir – but we'll get him – don't you worry yourself, sir.'

'I'm worried about my *dog*,' said Mr Kaye. 'I was very fond of him. That thief deserves to – to . . .' And then he saw Jack, and stopped. 'What do you want, Jack?' he said. 'Heard about my poor pup?'

'Yes, sir,' said Jack. 'I came to say I'm very sorry. Is there anything I can do for you, sir?'

'Well, that's nice of you,' said Mr Kaye. 'Come in. I'll tell you about Sasha – that's the pup. It's a mystery to me how he was stolen – a mystery. He wouldn't go anywhere with anyone, except me – and he was getting a big dog, you know – I mean, if anyone tried to take him by force, he'd fly at them.'

He took Jack into his sitting-room, and showed him a photograph of Sasha.

'Lovely, isn't he?' he said. 'I'm offering a large

reward for him. I paid over two hundred pounds for that pup, you know.'

'When did he disappear?' asked Jack.

'Last night – about half-past six,' said Mr Kaye. 'It was pitch-dark, and had been snowing. I let Sasha out for a bit, in the front garden – but when I called him, he didn't come. I hunted and hunted for him, took my torch out – and all I found were Sasha's paw-marks – and some very large footprints in the snow in my front garden. The police tell me it's been just the same with the other stolen dogs – some large-footed fellow comes along when a dog is let out for a short run – and the dog is never heard of again. Not a bark or a growl did I hear.'

'Anyone call on you yesterday evening?' asked Jack.

'Not that I know of,' said Mr Kaye. 'No – I don't remember asking anyone in last night. We were very quiet, my wife and I. It's nice of you to take such an interest, my boy, very nice.'

'Well, I do hope Sasha will turn up again,' said Jack. 'You're *sure* nobody called, sir?'

'I'd remember if I'd had any visitors, my boy – so would my wife – and we'd be *most* suspicious of them,' said Mr Kaye. 'Well, goodbye – and many thanks.'

111

Jack went down the drive to the front gate, frowning. He saw all kinds of footprints, both large and small – no good hoping to learn anything from those. A great many people seemed to have been walking all over the snowy garden, and the thief's footprints would be well and truly spoilt – all mixed up with everyone else's.

'This is a real puzzle that seems to have no solution,' thought Jack. 'Look at the way the thief took Scamper – no one saw him – no one heard him – and he wasn't any of the people who were known to come to the house. Who *was* he, and how did he manage to creep up to the farmhouse, watch for Scamper – and *get him*! And then take him away without a single person seeing him! It absolutely *beats* me! And yet there must be a simple answer to it all – an answer that even the police can't see! And WHERE are the dogs taken to? They simply disappear off the face of the earth, it seems. But they must be *somewhere* because obviously the thief only steals them because they are worth selling.'

Jack's thoughts came back to what he had heard the postman say – 'It'll be nice and dark then.' '*Nice and dark*' – why did the postman and his sister think that darkness was desirable? Could he *possibly* be in league with the thieves? After all, it was soon after he had said the night was 'nice and dark' that Sasha, Mr Kaye's Alsatian pup had been stolen.

'It obviously can't be the postman who is the thief,' thought Jack. 'He's little, not big – his feet are small and wouldn't make large prints in the snow – he adores dogs, and presumably wouldn't wish to steal them from their comfortable homes – and he couldn't POSSIBLY have taken away Scamper, because, if he had, someone would have seen Scamper running beside him. All the same – I think I'll go to Postie's house this afternoon, and have a little snoop round. I suppose he *might* have a cellar to hide dogs in. No – I'm getting silly. That tiny cottage *couldn't* have a cellar.'

He set off to the cottage about four o'clock that afternoon. Nobody was there. The front door and back door were both locked. Postie was obviously out on his rounds – Liz, his sister, was probably shopping. It really would be a good chance to poke round a bit.

'Not that I expect to find anything that will help,' said Jack to himself. 'I'm probably on a real wild-goose chase. I hope Postie or his sister don't come back and catch me. I'd get into real trouble then.'

He looked all round the little garden. He tried the handle of the garden shed, but it was locked. He peeped in at the kitchen window. He felt extremely guilty all the time and half-ashamed of himself. Whatever would his father say if he saw him? Then he remembered old Matt the shepherd and his sorrow for his lost collie – and thought of Peter and Janet, and their tears for Scamper.

'It's no good – I just *must* discover all I can that might be of help,' he thought.

He went back to the little shed, and peered through the small, dirty window, switching on his torch. It was difficult to see anything clearly at first, but after a while his eyes grew used to the shadows inside the shed, and he could make out some flower-pots, an old broom – and something else – something rather surprising! Yes, VERY surprising!

Jack stared and stared – and then suddenly heard a noise that made him stop staring and rush to climb over the fence at the end of the garden, and get away. A car had just driven up to the cottage gate – Jack heard the engine purr, and then stop. He caught a glimpse of it, in the light of a nearby lamp-post – a red van – gosh, it was the post-office van, that delivered parcels – Postie must have come back home to have a cup of tea! Jack fled away over the field at the back of Postie's garden, and disappeared. What a narrow escape! Another few seconds, and he would have been caught! Whew!

Eighteen

Well done, Jack

JACK raced home at top speed, his mind in a whirl. He couldn't forget what he had seen in that shed. He must tell someone, he must. If what he had seen meant what he thought it did, the great Dog Mystery was solved!

He bumped into Susie and Bony at the gate, and Susie caught hold of him.

'What's the matter? Why do you look so excited? You've *got* to tell me!'

Jack shook himself free. Goodness, he certainly couldn't cope with Susie just now. He'd better go up to the farm – yes, he *must* see Peter and Janet, even though he no longer belonged to the Secret Seven.

So, to Susie's anger and amazement, he shot off down the road, and then raced up to the farm, panting for all he was worth. He hammered on the front door.

'Good gracious – it's you, Jack – whatever's the matter?' said Peter, opening the door.

'Peter – it's important,' gasped Jack. 'I believe I know who the dog-thief is. Where's your father?'

'In the study,' said Peter, his eyes nearly falling out of his head. 'Quick – this way.'

Soon Jack was standing in the study, with a most surprised family listening to him.

'I think I know who stole Scamper!' he said. 'In fact, I'm CERTAIN!'

'Who?' said the children's father, sharply.

'The *postman* – old Postie!' said Jack. There was an amazed silence, and then Peter spoke.

'Impossible!' he said. 'Isn't it, Dad? The police say that the man had very large feet, and made big, deep footprints – and he probably had a van to take away the dogs.'

'The postman is very small with tiny feet,' said Mother.

'Well, I'll tell you what I saw in his shed a little while ago,' said Jack. 'I saw a HUGE pair of boots – really enormous! Now what would Postie want with *those*? They certainly weren't the right size for *his* small feet – so it's my guess that he wore them when he went out in the snow to steal Snowy – and to steal Shadow, up on the snowy hills. In fact, to steal *any* dog on a snowy night – leaving huge footprints behind to mislead everyone. I bet if you got hold of thosc boots, and looked at the copies of the footprints that the police have, they'd match EXACTLY!'

'But what about *Scamper*?' said Peter. 'Scamper wasn't stolen in the snow – he just disappeared. We *know* he didn't go with Postie, or he'd have been seen walking down to the village with him.'

'Did Postie bring any parcels for you yesterday?' asked Jack, and saw Mother nod her head. 'Right! Then he must have used the parcels *delivery* van – he could easily have patted Scamper's head, and made him follow him to the van – pushed him in, slammed the door – and driven off with him. No-body would know. Scamper loved him, so he probably wouldn't even have barked. I bet he's used that post-office van to shove dogs into plenty of times. I guess he took it up the road that runs alongside the sheepfields the day he left a letter at the hut for old Matt – and took Shadow off with him then. He'd say, "Come along, Shadow," and Shadow would follow him to the van – he'd get a push to send him inside – and slam would go the van door. Easy!'

'This is all very serious,' said the children's father. 'We must be very, very careful that you are right, Jack. Are you quite *sure* that you saw those boots? I didn't think of the post-office van, of course – Postie might quite well have taken Scamper away in it – the dog would follow him anywhere, he knew that Postie was a friend of the family.'

'My guess is that he threw down drugged meat to dogs he wouldn't be able to persuade into the van, waited till they dropped asleep – and then carried them there,' said Jack. 'You know how the police said there were scuffly patches of snow – well, they'd be made when he dragged away the dog.'

'Astounding!' said the children's father. 'Yes, it fits. It all fits. Yes, yes – he'd persuade some dogs to follow him to the van – and shut them in – and the others he would drug – and then drag or carry them to the van. Then off he could go with them – I wonder where?'

'The police will make him say,' said Mother. 'What a wicked fellow he is to cause such trouble and heart-break. Poor old Matt now – he seems to have aged terribly since Shadow was stolen.'

'Mother, he'll look all right again when he gets Shadow back,' cried Janet. 'Oh quick, let's do something. Let's make Postie tell us where he took the dogs. Has he *sold* Scamper? Can we buy him back? Quick, Daddy, quick, Mother.'

'Can't we go and tell the police straightaway?'

said Peter. '*They* ought to go and make Postie own up, and confess everything, oughtn't they?'

'Yes,' said his father. He turned to Jack and patted him on the back. 'You'll have to come with me, Jack. You've done well – very well. You've succeeded where everyone else has failed. The police will want to know everything you can tell them. Come along.'

'Can we come too?' cried Peter.

'No,' said his father. 'Only Jack. We'll go this very minute. Mother, telephone the police and tell them we're coming, and why.'

He went out into the darkening evening with a beaming Jack. Peter rushed after Jack and caught hold of his arm.

'Oh, Jack! You *are* a marvel! Thank you, thank you for coming with such good news.'

Jack grinned and went off with Peter's father. What an excitement – WHAT an excitement! Good old Jack! Good old everybody!

Nineteen

All's well again!

PETER and Janet and their mother could hardly wait for Dad and Jack to return. It seemed AGES before the car could be heard purring up the drive. Janet heard a bark as it drew up, and yelled in delight.

'SCAMPER! It's SCAMPER!' And sure enough it was – dear, silky old Scamper, his ears flopping up and down as he rushed into the hall, his tail wagging nineteen to the dozen. He flung himself on the children, barking loudly in joy. In fact, he couldn't *stop* barking, and was most surprised to find that Janet's face was salty with happy tears, when he licked it.

'And here's SHADOW!' yelled Peter. 'Dad, you've got him too. Is he all right?'

'Perfectly – except that he moped for Matt,' said his father. 'My word, I shall look forward to seeing old Matt's face tomorrow.'

'No, Dad – let him go to Matt tonight,' begged Janet. 'He'll rush up the hills straight as an arrow

and find Matt for himself. Matt won't want anyone there when he first sees Shadow again.'

'You're right, Janet darling,' said her mother. 'Put Shadow out of doors, Dad. Let him go to Matt.'

So the door was opened – and the collie shot out like an arrow from a bow! He disappeared into the darkness of the evening, barking wildly.

'He's calling "Matt! Matt! Matt!"' said Janet. 'Oh, Scamper, darling, darling Scamper, I've missed you so. Oh, that horrible Postie – how DARE he steal dogs?'

'What happened when you took the police to Postie's house?' Peter asked Jack.

'Well, nothing very much, really,' said Jack. 'Liz, Postie's sister, was simply terrified when we arrived, and blurted out everything. Postie wasn't there then – he came in later – but by that time Liz had told us that when he went out into the snow at night, he *did* wear those enormous boots I saw, to make people think that the dog-thief was a great big man. He stamped his feet hard into the ground, to make deep prints, as if he were very heavy.'

'Most of the dogs came to him willingly, according to Liz,' said his father. 'Others he drugged as we thought, by giving them meat with pills in. The odd thing is that *every* dog adores him – he had no trouble at all.'

'Where did he take them?' asked Mother.

'To a friend of his, four miles away, who is a vet – it's his second cousin, I believe. And this fellow kept the dogs till all the excitement had died down, and then quietly sold them. Postie must have made a lot of money.'

'Where is Postie now?' asked Janet.

'In a prison-cell,' said her father grimly, 'and he

deserves to be well punished. Dog-stealing is a wicked thing – a cruel thing. Thank goodness that Postie's cousin treated the dogs well. Postie used the post-office van to take Scamper away – and many other dogs – and drove them straight to his cousin – so no wonder they seemed to disappear off the face of the earth.'

Mother suddenly put her arms round the smiling, silent Jack, and gave him a hug.

'You shall have a reward,' she said, 'a huge reward – the nicest present you can possibly think of! Clever old Jack! Fancy you snooping round and spotting what those great boots really meant! What shall we give him as a reward, Dad?'

'I don't want ANYTHING!' said Jack, going red. 'My reward is seeing how glad Scamper was to come home! And seeing your faces when he came running indoors!'

Janet went to whisper in Peter's ear, and he nodded eagerly. He turned to Jack.

'Jack – will you do me a favour, please?' he said. 'A very great favour?'

'Of course,' said Jack, at once.

'Then please will you allow me to pin this on to your coat?' said Peter, and pulled out of his pocket the S.S. badge that Jack had refused to take back.

'PLEASE, Jack. We've missed you so. We're all sorry now. We'll have a WONDERFUL meeting tomorrow, down in the shed, and tell everyone your great story – you'll have to tell it yourself – about taking the police out to the shed and everything.'

'All right,' said Jack, his eyes shining as Peter pinned the S.S. badge to his coat. 'I've missed you all too. Now we can be the Secret *Seven* again! Goodness – won't Susie be surprised! I'm longing to see her face! Scamper will be at the meeting too, won't he?'

'Wuff-wuff, wuff-wuff!' said Scamper at once, wagging his tail.

'He says, "Of course, of course!"' said Janet, and she was right!

'And now we'll all have something to eat,' said Mother. 'This kind of thing makes me very hungry. Scamper, go and ask Mrs Simmons for the largest bone she has.'

Scamper trotted out to the kitchen at once, and was thrilled to have a great welcome from Mrs Simmons. He came back carrying a most enormous bone, and looked very pleased with himself indeed. He took it on the mat to gnaw.

'He hasn't forgotten his manners,' said Mother, pleased. 'I wonder how dear old Shadow is getting on. He must be half-way up the snowy hills by now.'

Yes – Shadow was on his way to Matt, the master he loved. He was bounding over the snow, up the hills to where the sheep were kept. The stars were out now, and their faint light shone down on the long, lean body loping steadily up the hill. If Matt had grieved for Shadow, the collie had certainly grieved for Matt. He had eaten nothing since he had been stolen, and was as lean as a greyhound.

Up he went, and on and on. Ah – there was his master's hut, outlined against the night sky, at the top of the hill. A dim light showed in the tiny window.

All's well again!

Shadow had no breath left to bark, for he had run up the long, long hill without a moment's rest. He came to the hut and hurled himself against the door, panting loudly.

Matt was startled. 'Who's that?' he cried. And then he heard a whine – a whine that made him leap at once from his old wooden chair. Shadow scraped at the bottom of the door, and began to bark. Matt's hands were shaking with joy as he unlocked the door.

'SHADOW, old dog! You've come back to me!' said Matt, in a wondering, trembling voice. Shadow flung himself on the old shepherd, licking him, loving him, whining, his tail waving and wagging without a stop.

Matt sank down on his chair, and Shadow at once took up his old place, sitting close by the shepherd, his head on his knees, looking up at him with loving brown eyes. Matt put his wrinkled old hand on the dog's soft head.

'I missed you, old friend, I missed you,' he said. 'Like a brother I grieved for you, and my heart was full of sorrow. Where have you come from, this cold night of stars? Did you guess I was a-waiting for you every hour of the day and night? But I knew you'd come, old dog, I knew you'd come. We'll lie us down to sleep in peace tonight – just you and me together.'

Goodbye, old Matt and Shadow; goodbye, Scamper and the Secret Seven. It's good to know you're happy once again!